I0668807

The Train That Had Wings

Selected Short Stories of
M. MUKUNDAN

Translated from the Malayalam by Donald R. Davis, Jr.

The Centers for South and Southeast Asian Studies
The University of Michigan
Ann Arbor

Open access edition funded by the National Endowment for the Humanities/
Andrew W. Mellon Foundation Humanities Open Book Program.

Copyright © by the Centers for South and Southeast Asian Studies 2005

Published in the United States of America by
The Centers for South and Southeast Asian Studies
Manufactured in the United States of America

2008   2007   2006   2005   4   3   2   1

A CIP catalog record for this book for the British Library is forthcoming.

Library of Congress Cataloging-in-Publication is applied for.
Cloth ISBN: 0-89148-090-0
Paper ISBN: 0-89148-091-9

ISBN 978-0-89148-090-7 (hardcover)
ISBN 978-0-89148-091-4 (paper)
ISBN 978-0-472-12771-9 (ebook)
ISBN 978-0-472-90167-8 (open access)

Contents

Preface

Why I Like Mukundan . . . and Hate Him, Too

A five-and-a-half year old's social angst, flying trains with wings, the tragic life of houseflies, breast milk addicts, psychedelic oceans, and a rich man urinating in a cremation ground. These disparate images are all concoctions of the peculiar imagination of M. Mukundan. They are part and parcel of Mukundan's own ocean of stories, which includes both novels and short stories.

Reading a Mukundan story is not an art; it is a calculus. No special training is required, if you are willing to lose your prejudices, your traditions, and your self for as long as it takes to finish the story. You must add up the world without these refuges. Some writers play with humanity's prejudices and traditions in order to tell their tale and make their impact. In Mukundan's short stories, however, cultural heritage and biases are flip-flopped, warped, stretched out like taffy. Mukundan's world is certainly our world, but not exactly. Sometimes it is more intense; sometimes more cruel; always more raw. It is our world without the skin and muscle, but the blood is the same.

A Mukundan story is not a satisfying meal. When you finish the last word of a Mukundan story, there is rarely an immediate gratification, followed by a temporary digestion of its significance. But the story works on your mind, and as it does it ceases to annoy you, to thwart you. It takes on a new meaning as its images, reversals, and personalities continually recreate its significance. And just when you think you've figured it out, you haven't.

Mukundan's commitment to modernism, his Western education, his familiarity with Western languages, especially English and French, his diplomatic career in the French Embassy in Delhi, and his commitment to modernism make his stories somewhat easier to translate into English than more regionalized stories from Kerala which are often full of unfamiliar images, untranslatable words, and highly idiomatic colloquialisms. Thus, the Western reader will feel very much at home with Mukundan's references to Surrealist painters, Argentinian revolutionaries, and Minimalist poets.

This is not to say that Mukundan's stories, and especially his novels, do not also taste of the flavor of Kerala and its unique cultural heritage. The settings for some of the stories are the towns and villages of Kerala. Glimpses of daily life and images peculiar to Kerala, especially to Mukundan's native Mahe, the former French colony, are common. At the same time, the cosmopolitan character of Mukundan's short stories differs from his principal novels, two of which have already appeared in fine English translations (see Suggestions for Futher Reading). The latter are renowned for their portrayals of life in Kerala. Indeed, Mukundan is best known for his compelling descriptions of life in culturally heterogeneous Mahe. One novel in particular, *On the Banks of the Mayyazhi River*, has won Mukundan his place in the history of Malayalam literature. To date, his short stories have not received the same accolades as his novels. But the risks Mukundan takes in his short stories merit an audience beyond speakers of Malayalam because they represent a excellent example of the largely unknown achievements of contemporary authors in India's numerous vernacular languages and because of their profound impact on subsequent writing in Malayalam itself. It is this conviction that led me to take on the translation of the short stories in this collection.

I first began to read Mukundan's short stories in 1995 on a recommendation from a local bookseller in Calicut. I quickly discovered that the inviting simplicity of Mukundan's language is sharply contrasted to the seductive complexity and depth of his ideas. While Mukundan's use of language is relatively easier for readers of the original Malayalam to understand, it still presents many of the usual difficulties of translation in an English rendition. Simple, pithy phrases are frequently the most difficult to capture in the target language with the same force. In such situations, I have often had to change the literal nuance or the image given in the original in favor of a similar nuance, more familiar image, or simply more powerful wording in English. In the end, I have rendered Mukundan's stories into conversational American English. In so doing, I have tried to produce a translation that is palatable to my intended audience of American readers. Ultimately, whether in Malayalam or English, the stories are those of M. Mukundan, and I have simply tried to present them to an audience that does not read Malayalam.

Donald R. Davis, Jr.
Madison, WI

Introduction

Before the 1960s, Malayalam literature, whether poetry, novel, or short story, had been dominated by a parochialism centered on the lives and experiences of Kerala, a small state of palm trees, trading ports, and paddy fields in southwestern India. Most literary productions from this period in Kerala's history depicted scenes, people, habits, and conflicts native to Kerala—and only to Kerala. On the one hand, it is only natural that a language spoken almost exclusively in this small geographic area would produce a literature focused on that region. On the other hand, one could say that Kerala has been a sort of imaginative prison for Malayalam, beyond the walls of which not much is written in Malayalam. By this, I do not mean that all Malayalam fiction of this period was set in Kerala, though this is largely true, but rather that Malayalam as a language was not often employed to investigate or explore cultural worlds beyond those of its native provenance.

In the early 1960s, a small group of Malayalam authors broke these parochial bonds by creating new styles of fiction and poetry that had little to do with traditional Kerala themes. Names like Anand (P. Sachidanandan), O. V. Vijayan, Kakkanadan, and M. Mukundan are prominent in this group of modernist authors who diverged from the realistic and romantic prose of their predecessors. Most of these authors are still writing today and continue to challenge the limitations of theme, setting, style, and so on felt in earlier periods of modern Malayalam literature.

As one of the most successful modernist authors in Malayalam, M. Mukundan (b. 1942) has acquired a considerable following among Kerala literati as well as the Kerala populace generally. Mukundan is best known for his compelling descriptions of life in the culturally heterogeneous small former French colony called Mahe in present-day Kerala. His most beloved works are his novels—*On the Banks of the Mayyazhi River, God's Mischief,* and, most recently, *The Lamentations of Kesavan.* In my opinion, however, the experiments with language, the images, and the style of Mukundan's short stories have impacted Malayalam literature to a greater extent than his somewhat more conventional, more popular novels.

In the course of this introduction to Mukundan's stories, I will consider first the general themes of the stories and then contextualize Mukundan's work in relation to other Malayalam writers and to the larger literary world. Mukundan, like many Malayalis in the 1950s and 60s, read and was influenced by European and South American revolutionary literature, from the high literature and philosophy of Jean-Paul Sartre to the militant Marxist essays and speeches of Che Guevara. As a result, despite their setting in India, the general themes of Mukundan's stories center on characters, events, and settings that will be familiar to Western readers. Mukundan revisits the common themes of anomie and captivity that appear in many modernist and existentialist texts throughout the 1960s. His twists on the perils of industrialism, bureaucracy, religion, and poverty give his modernist vision a unique perspective that does not derive slavishly from Western models.

Indeed, to my mind, Mukundan's intertwining of modernist themes and Indian contexts constitutes his greatest contribution to Malayalam literature. To be sure, Mukundan's contemporaries also pushed Malayalam literature in new directions both stylistically and substantively. For example, one could consider O. V. Vijayan's stylistically pathbreaking *The Legends of*

Khasak or the alienation and political rhetoric of Anand's *The Refugees* or Kakkanadan's *World of the Dogs*. Their contributions, on the other hand, speak to other dilemmas and negotiations of modernity, such as technology, loss of tradition, and political power. Mukundan's work, on the other hand, articulates a vision of modernity as cosmopolitanism—a shared but tragically compromised humanity. Mukundan offers us a cosmopolitanism of suffering and emotional alienation, suggesting that humans are united by experiences of personal loss, social awkwardness, institutional oppression, and libidinous evil. Mukundan's genius is to write stories about Kerala and about India that feel like stories about almost anywhere. This was something new for Malayalam literature and can be seen most easily in the tiny stories of Mukundan.

In fact, the singular contribution of Mukundan to Malayalam literature was to pull Malayalam out of its link with Kerala and its associated images, themes, history, people, and lifestyles. Mukundan liberated Malayalam from its parochial bonds and helped make it possible to write a truly cosmopolitan story in the language of Kerala. By discarding scenes, values, and characters typically or exclusively connected with Kerala, Mukundan infused his short stories with a cosmopolitanism that rarely appeared in Malayalam short stories before him.

What is most interesting for a Western reader, however, is the manner in which Mukundan's cosmopolitan and modernist commitments express a different perspective on contemporary life, especially its darker side, than is typically available in European and American works from the same period. What we gain, at least in part, from reading Mukundan is the important and obvious, but often overlooked, fact that Kerala and India possess a modernity, indeed multiple forms of it, that may differ from those found in Western settings. That modernity, for all its academic contestations, took and takes different forms is a fact that had not been made clear until recently, but Mukundan in these stories offers us an early sense of what present-day authors, critics, and academics now discuss with verve. Through his stories, Mukundan interprets modernity in terms of a cosmopolitan existentialism, a recurrent assertion that humans everywhere share emotional and psychological pressures that transcend cultural boundaries—an assertion, no doubt, informed by Mukundan's own unusually diverse education, cultural influences, and geographic locations.

General Themes of Mukundan's Stories

Two prominent themes in Mukundan's short stories elucidate some of the literary devices he uses to allow Malayalam to speak of more than just Kerala and to reach for a way to express this cosmopolitanism. The first theme is anomie, or a person's sense of lost purpose, identity, or value. In contrast to the chaos of anomie, the second theme focuses on a rigid sense of captivity, or being stuck in burdensome, tedious, or morally bankrupt social roles or situations. Despite the apparent incongruity of the two themes, they actually work together in Mukundan's stories to capture the feeling of both personal and social failure in the modern world.

We begin then with anomie and with what is probably Mukundan's most famous short story—"Radha, Just Radha." When it was published in the early 1960s, "Radha, Just Radha" set a standard for modernist or existentialist stories in Malayalam that, some would say, has yet to be surpassed. The story opens with the young woman, Radha, approaching her boyfriend at a bus stop. Although she knows Suresh and recounts their time together "in the salty whispers of the wind" the previous day, Suresh does not acknowledge her, nor even recognize her. And so begins the painful encounter between Radha and Suresh that turns into a public humiliation as Suresh repeatedly insists that he does not know this young woman, eventually shouting at her to leave him alone and to stop embarrassing him. Radha does leave and walks home past

Bhaskaran's tea stall, but neither Bhaskaran nor Kannan Master recognize her as she passes by. At last, she reaches home where her father reads the daily paper. As with the others, her father and her mother don't recognize her—at first taking pity on her, then trying to ignore her as though she were insane. Radha protests that she is their daughter, but they deny it. She tries to run to her room, but they block her. In the end, she is defeated and forced to leave with the parting words: "Where will I go, Mommy? I have no one except you and Daddy . . . ." And with that, she departs, the world lost to her, as "the birds, the trees, the ocean gusts, the sky, the land—in a single voice, they sang: You are not Radha. We know you not."

The beauty of this Mukundan story, and indeed most Mukundan stories, derives from its failure to reach a neat conclusion, to mean something specific, or to moralize indiscriminately. Certainly the theme of anomie stands out in Radha's predicament–she has literally lost her identity, her place in the world. But what has actually happened is unclear. Still less clear is what Radha's failure to be recognized means. Is there a moral to the story? We could easily supply one, but would it be *the* moral? The lack of clarity thus tells us more about our own presuppositions in reading the story than about Mukundan's intentions while writing it.

Although "Radha, Just Radha" is set in Kerala, the setting itself is simply a backdrop to a story that could have been placed almost anywhere. In fact, the main effect added by the Kerala setting is the opposite of most Malayalam short stories, which use typically Keralite lifestyles and settings to explore universal themes of love, loss, and so on. In the case of "Radha, Just Radha," by contrast, Mukundan takes an emotion that at first seems inappropriate to the Kerala context, the cosmopolitan and typically modernist thematic emotion of anomie, and shows how that emotion can live in the surprisingly provincial setting of Kerala. One doesn't expect young Malayali women to experience the same sense of lost identity or disconnection as one of Sartre's or Kafka's characters, but this is precisely what Mukundan challenges us to imagine. Mukundan often combines such portrayals of lost identity with depictions of characters oppressively imprisoned in their social, occupational, religious, or family lives.

Such combinations lead to the second theme of captivity. By captivity, I mean a sense of being held captive in a relationship, a job, a family, or any other social role. Modernist writers have exposed and explored social restraints and societal pressures to conform at least since the early twentieth century and the modernist reaction to Victorian morality. One of Mukundan's most powerful indictments of this sense of captivity in the world is his story called "Tonsured Life." Exactly which social restraints are being indicted is never clear. What *is* clear in this story is that religious leaders exacerbate the problem of captivity.

The unnamed narrator of "Tonsured Life" works in a Delhi office. This typical day he is busy at work when his receptionist and sometime lover calls him to say that someone is waiting to see him, a holy man with the intimidating name Lakshman-lal Pyari-lal Pandit-ji. Having no special interest in religious matters, the narrator wonders what this person could want with him. Eventually, however, he decides to meet the pandit. Immediately, the pandit starts ordering the narrator around, commanding him to go outside. For no apparent reason, other than perhaps curiosity, the narrator obeys and follows the pandit outside where a religious procession, a *yatra,* awaits him. The pandit calls a barber over, not merely a barber in the usual sense, but a religious specialist who performs tonsuring rites at temples or festivals. The barber proceeds to shave the narrator bald, tonsuring not only his head, but his heart, his soul, and indeed his life. Shaved, and one might say consecrated, he is paraded through the city on the back of an ass. His former lovers, the children, the mothers, and the poor of the city see him and call him "son of a pig," a cruel epithet akin to "son of bitch" or "motherfucker" in English. Eventually the procession stops so that the drummers and bell ringers can get tea—everyone except the narrator. As he rests, the pandit takes out a Bible to read during the respite and later the Koran as well. The religious procession goes on all day with the participants frequently stopping for food and drink. The narrator is parched and fatigued, his tonsured head sunburned. Finally, at dusk the procession stops near the Red Fort. Everyone disperses. The narrator summons up the strength to ask what the readers have wanted to know all along: "Why this punishment, Pandit-ji?" The pandit reminds the narrator of an old man who had approached the narrator's home for a glass of water. The narrator remembers well that he had invited the old man in and had given him several glasses of cool water and a place to escape the heat, after which the old man thanked him and went on his way. In a fit of rage prompted by this act, Pandit-ji barks at the narrator, "Why did you give this man water? Who are you to give water to the thirsty?" Pandit-ji then spits in the narrator's face and leaves him lying half-dead in the dark.

In "Tonsured Life," Mukundan indicts religion, or at least religious leaders, with a critique of their self-serving desire to control even such quotidian good deeds as giving a poor man a glass of water. The image of Pandit-ji spitting in the narrator's face because he dared to do something kind, purely out of human compassion and not for religious duty, strikes me as a poignant statement of the captivity we experience, even when we think we are in control.

While religious elites have been satirized for centuries in India for their hypocrisy and exploitation of "the masses," Mukundan's criticism is more cosmopolitan in scope, mentioning Hindu, Christian, and Muslim scriptures. He directs his satiric story toward religion in general, not merely to a particular group of hypocritical religious leaders. By indicting religion in such a pervasive way, Mukundan challenges every reader to question the influence of potentially pernicious religious leaders over their lives. Of course, Mukundan's story brings this malevolent side of religion into unrealistic relief, but the twist at the end is nevertheless most effective. Captivity is a symptom of a modern disease that is universal, not one limited to

Delhi or Kerala. Mukundan's exploration of captivity complements the theme of anomie by showing the paradox of "being stuck" and "being lost" at the same time. The psychological and emotional movement toward a sense of captivity or anomie is often symbolized in Mukundan's story by walking. And so we turn to the walking motif.

The Motif of Walking and the Shortness of the Story

Walking for Mukundan signals transformation, passing from one moral, philosophical, or existential state or status into another—usually not for the better. In fact, when a character or group of characters starts walking in a Mukundan story, something big is about to happen. People walk to their destinies in a Mukundan story. They rarely drive or fly or go by bullock cart.

A single example suffices to illustrate how Mukundan uses this motif of walking to structure his short stories in a way that differs from other authors in Malayalam literature. It is worth noting, however, that the previous examples of anomie and captivity also contain this walking motif. Radha walks through her familiar world only to be completely unrecognized by any of her friends, neighbors, or family. The narrator of "Tonsured Life" follows Pandit-ji out of his office. Although he himself rides an ass through the streets of Delhi, everyone else walks, signaling perhaps that he is not in control of his destiny, but must be escorted there, as the theme of captivity would suggest.

Another characteristic example of Mukundan's walking motif comes from the story called simply "Piss." It is the story of the death of a man named Kumaran Nayar, who was a well-to-do moneylender and a man feared for his collection techniques. Some say it was spirits who got him; others say it was the Naxalites. But the narrator of the story boldly declares that it was neither. At this point we flash back.

The narrator has a problem. A friend, Kannan, has asked him for a small hundred-rupee loan to pay for the care of his wife, who has just given birth by C-section. Unfortunately, the banks have already closed for the Saturday holiday, and Kannan needs the money before Monday to prevent his wife from potentially losing her life. The narrator has the money in the bank, but he can't get it in time. He asks his wife if she has any money tucked away, but she doesn't. So, he is stuck without a way to help his friend as he promised he would. Finally, his wife suggests that he ask Kumaran Nayar, who always has money to lend. The narrator resists because he has never borrowed money and knows Kumaran Nayar's reputation. With no alternative, however, he eventually acquiesces.

As he prepares to leave, a workman named Kelappan informs him that Madhavan, an out-of-towner and something of a lovable neighborhood bum, has died. Kelappan has just dug the hole for Madhavan's cremation. So, the narrator sets out for Kumaran Nayar's home to borrow the money. As he arrives, he sees Kumaran Nayar rushing off somewhere. The narrator shouts to stop him, but he turns and walks off down the alley. Through the streets and alleys, the narrator follows Kumaran Nayar, humiliated to be chasing someone to borrow money but always remembering the face of his friend's wife. Finally, after a winding series of twists and turns, the walking leads down an alley toward the cremation ground. Kumaran Nayar enters the cremation ground where the deceased Madhavan's corpse is burning in a mound of earth. He rants at Madhavan for dying before he repaid the money he owed Kumaran Nayar. In this fit of rage, Kumaran Nayar lifts his dhoti and starts to piss on the smoking mound. Incensed by this horrific sight, the narrator himself loses control: "All I remember is leaping forward with the stone. When I came to my senses, I saw Kumaran Nayar lying face down in his own blood and piss."

This final image of Kumaran Nayar's corpse drenched in the symbols of his own sin haunts both the narrator and the reader. The image marks the culmination of a man's transformation from ordinary family man to killer—a transformation precipitated by a walk he didn't want to take. The walk opens the narrator's eyes, allows him to see the cruel reality of the neighborhood around him. As in so many other Mukundan stories, the walking motif here signifies people leaving behind complacence, ignorance, and innocence. The world they find outside of the comfort of their homes is rarely secure, comfortable, or kind. Indeed, it is dangerous, disturbed, and cruel, but it is real. And Mukundan never shies away from showing the blood and bones of raw human life. Whether they are forced to or choose to, many Mukundan characters walk to their destinies, leaving behind their naive views of the world, encountering instead a world they didn't know before or didn't want to know.

This single example of the walking motif hardly does justice to Mukundan's sophisticated deployment of this recurring symbol of transformation. Walking in Mukundan's short stories functions as one of those repeated acts of genius that often arise in great artistic and literary productions—the choppy brush-strokes of Monet, the G-chord bass run of the blues, or the simple lines of Frank Lloyd Wright. Mukundan is, of course, not the first or only author to describe characters walking, but his repeated use of this motif becomes characteristic of his style. Indeed, the shortness of Mukundan's short stories is in large part attributable to the fact that many of them center on one long walk. The events surrounding or during that walk are often the bulk of the story and signal the important frame the walking motif supplies to many of Mukundan's stories.

More importantly, Mukundan uses this walking motif precisely at those moments of transformation that seem oddly unlike the traditional Kerala that so permeates the intense nostalgia of popular sentiment and literary reflection one encounters among Malayalis. And this is really the point, for I believe that Mukundan uses the themes of anomie and captivity and the motif of walking primarily to explore broader questions about such "un-Kerala" issues as existentialism, modernism, and cosmopolitanism—issues that he wants to suggest are not foreign to Kerala at all. Chronologically speaking, Mukundan may not be the first Malayalam author to explore imaginative worlds beyond Kerala in his work, but he is, in my estimation, the most successful and the most systematic in trying to write about worlds and people whose problems are not Kerala-bound, not tied to the breakdown of Nayar family structures, the struggle for independence, or the plight of fishing communities. Mukundan's characters may as well live in New York or Berlin or Tokyo, for their dilemmas and experiences mirror those of an industrial, urban, and secular society.

When Malayalis—at least the ones I know, whether they live in rural villages, urban ports, outside of the state, or abroad—speak of Kerala, they focus first on the paddy fields, the myriad rivers, the lush green hills, and the simplicity of life that they imagine to be at the heart of Kerala. In many ways, this is the only Kerala that is visible, due in large part to the aggressive cultivation of this image in public forums, governmental advertising, and, significantly, a still large proportion of Malayalam literature. The magic of Mukundan is to suggest that even this provincialized Kerala feels these modern, cosmopolitan burdens in its agricultural, semirural, and often religious life.

Contextualizing Mukundan's Stories

Situating Mukundan's stories in Malayalam literature and more generally in the literature of India and the world is more than a matter of identifying his apparent debts, allegiances, and influence. Mukundan's debts are numerous and include both his social-realist predecessors in Malayalam and the early modernist authors of Europe. From the former's dense description of life in Kerala, Mukundan acquired a felicitous capacity to paint a scene with words, to capture a detail of the story or a verbal nuance that offers the reader a brief, but profound, sense of the narrative moment. From the latter's stylistic and substantive experiments with language, emotion, and sense of self, Mukundan innovated on the Malayalam short story genre by infusing it with a sense of modernity and personal alienation that was missing from earlier writing in Malayalam. Beyond this novel integration of two literary worlds, however, Mukundan offers us something else, a glimpse of humanity and a vision of life that transcends the commonplace and the commonsensical. One way to demonstrate the distinctive literary contribution of Mukundan is to compare his approach to a subject with that of other authors.

For more than two hundred years, the life of scavengers in India has both repulsed and fascinated foreign and indigenous writers in their descriptions of life in India. Scavengers, of course, are the men and women who collect the waste and junk from Indian neighborhoods, who sweep the streets, and who, most famously, clean the toilets, both public and private, of a large part of the subcontinent. Several well-known Indian authors have taken up the life of scavengers as a fictional subject. Mukundan also deals with the scavengers' life in the story "I, the Scavenger." By comparing Mukundan's story with the treatments of scavengers by Mulk Raj Anand, whose novel *Untouchable* became one of best known early works of English fiction from late colonial India, and Takazhi Sivasankara Pillai, whose novel *Scavenger's Son* has been lauded as one of the great works of realist Malayalam literature, we can begin to see the kind of unexpected worldview and sense of humanity found in Mukundan's stories.

In 1934, Mulk Raj Anand found a fan in E. M. Forster, who championed his short novel, *Untouchable,* because Anand had come to "understand a tragedy he did not share" (Anand 1940: vii). The publication of *Untouchable* put a human face on the lives of the scavengers and sweepers of India. The novel tells the story of Bakha, an Anglophile young scavenger who likes to dress in European clothes and mimic the English soldiers he sees. The central conflict of the story occurs when Bakha accidentally bumps into a middle-class man on the street as he savors a private moment of decadence in the syrup candy he had selfishly purchased. The touch of such an untouchable was considered extremely polluting and the offended man proceeds to cause a scene and gather a crowd to berate Bakha for his crime. Bakha has no choice but to suffer impotently the insults and slaps of the crowd. As he escapes the scene, Bakha thinks to himself, "The picture of the touched man stood in the forefront, among several indistinct faces, his bloodshot eyes, his little body with the sunken cheeks, his dry, thin lips, his ridiculously agitated manner, his abuse; and there was the circle of the crowd, jeering, scoffing, abusing, while he himself stood with joined hands in the center. 'Why was all this?' he asked himself . . . " (1940: 51). Bakha's plight is compounded by the ignominy cast on him by his own father. Despite this miserable situation, the story continues with Bakha experimenting with, but ultimately rejecting, the salvation offered him by a Christian missionary. Finally, he attends a rally for Gandhi at which he learns not only of the political hope offered by Gandhi to the untouchables, but also about the technological promise of flush toilets as the end of scavenging. These hopes close a story that focuses on the wretched lives of scavengers who are portrayed as yearning for social and economic equality.

Untouchable is notable for being one of the earliest attempts by an upper-caste Indian writer to capture the emotions and aspirations of the lower classes of Indian society. Much like *Untouchable,* Thakazhi's *Scavenger's Son* departed from the standard literary works of the time which were "peopled with characters from the middle and upper levels of society." Indeed, R. E. Asher's description of *Scavenger's Son* applies equally well to *Untouchable:* "A novel which attempted to portray members of the very lowest stratum of society as if they were people capable of real human feelings was a very new departure" (x).

Malayalam literature of the 1940s and 1950s is replete with

stories of the changes and hardships of life in Kerala at the time—a fact that may be attributed in part to strength of the Socialist and Communist movements in Kerala and the desire, even perhaps the requirement, that all fiction should support this new vision. The period just before and just after the independence of India was officially declared in 1947 was a time of such social-realist novels in Malayalam. *Scavenger's Son,* as with most of Thakazhi's work, examines the lives of lower classes through a rich descriptive narrative coupled with complex, heart-wrenching plots. Thakazhi's description of the life and aspirations of the scavenger Chudalamuttu traces Chudalamuttu's sense of confinement and dissatisfaction with the degrading scavenger life. The principal theme of the novel is Chudalamuttu's desperation to escape the occupational, social, and physical confines of the scavenger community. "Must we be satisfied to live for ever as scavengers?" (35) he asks his new wife early in the story. Chudalamuttu tries to hide from his son the fact that theirs is a family of scavengers. The perils of the scavenger life seem inescapable, however, as both Chudalamuttu and his wife die in a cholera outbreak just as Chudalamuttu has connived and schemed to become the watchman at the cremation ground. He dies with dreams unfulfilled, as Thakazhi writes: "Chudalamuttu hoped that his son would not become a scavenger. He gave him a name that did not go with being a scavenger. The boy grew up ignorant of the meaning of the word 'scavenger.' The father used to be furious if he saw the child lying in dirt for even a short while. But today that child is a scavenger in Allepey town" (109). As a socialist, however, Thakazhi could not end with the inexorability of poverty and pollution. Thus, the final scene depicts Chudalamuttu's son, Mohanan, leading a revolutionary march to unionize the scavengers.

Both Anand and Thakazhi concentrate on the wretchedness, the desperation, and the suffering associated with the scavenger life and the scavenger community. Both novels contain characters who long to break free of the scavenger curse. At every turn, unfortunately, society keeps the scavengers in their place, mocks them, abuses them, and exploits them. From such representations, one certainly gets the impression that few things are worse in India than being a scavenger. Scavengers are miserable, oppressed, and eager to break the chains that bind.

How odd it seems then for Mukundan to describe the protagonist of his story, "I, the Scavenger," as feeling "tremendous joy" at becoming a scavenger. In a way, Mukundan picks up where Anand and Thakazhi left off. In a world so mired in poverty, even a job cleaning putrid public toilets is a kind of godsend. The scavengers in Mukundan's story are not the wretched of the earth. They are some of the lucky ones, some of the fortunate few who manage to have jobs at all, much less government jobs through the municipality. Consonant with the theme of captivity so prevalent in Mukundan's stories, even this scavenger's life is controlled by Mr. Shishupalan, whose influence over the scavenger extends even to death. Nevertheless, the implications of Mukundan's simple story push beyond the realistic portrayals of the scavenger life.

"I, the Scavenger" is both a more severe indictment of the injustices against and the oppression of scavengers in India and a more sensitive depiction of the humanity of the scavengers than either Anand's or Thakazhi's work. That scavengers would be happy to have their jobs suggests a world below the scavenging life that the reader is left to ponder without description. The unimaginable squalor and misery of this world is only dimly mirrored in Mukundan's portrayal of the scavenger life. At the same time, the security afforded by regular work as a scavenger permits the unnamed protagonist to make a home, to find a wife, to father a family. In other words, the human side of scavengers does not need to be shown by presenting them as pitiful victims of social injustice, but rather by portraying them in the experiences of the good life shared by rich and poor alike. In this way, Mukundan's story is more humane, in the sense of representing agency rather than just oppression, than the potentially victimizing representations of earlier stories about scavengers. Indian fiction, it seems, had to go through the phase of describing the lower classes as helpless, joyless, and unfulfilled. Mukundan's genius is to move beyond this phase by imagining what joy, achievement, and contentment mean to scavengers and how these emotions depend on the same life experiences shared by all people.

Mukundan's approach to the life of scavengers is but one example of his pushing Malayalam literature in a new direction, one that appropriates techniques and styles from both India and Europe to forge a truly novel vision of human life. The vision is at once psychological, philosophical, and anthropological in its observations on the emotive, intellectual, and cultural life of humanity. But it is not monolithic as Mukundan experiments with different styles ranging from a quasi-realistic story such as "Office" to the word-play and syntactical games of "They are Singing." Throughout this range of literary production, which continues to the present, the common contribution is an expansion of the horizon of Malayalam as a literary language. Given the tremendous contributions of his contemporaries, it may not be proper to speak of Malayalam before and after Mukundan, but I think it is fair to say that more than any other author in Malayalam, Mukundan has consistently pushed the boundaries of accepted literary practice, challenged the mores of the day, and carried Malayalam beyond the borders of Kerala into the sinews and synapses of human life.

REFERENCES

Anand, Mulk Raj. [1935] 1940. *Untouchable.* Preface by E.M. Forster. New York: Penguin.
Mukundan, M. [1982] 1995. *Mukandante Kathakal (Selected Stories by M. Mukundan).* 2nd ed. Kottayam: Current Books.
Pillai, Thakazhi Sivasankara. [1947] 1993. *Scavenger's Son (Tottiyute Makan).* Trans. R. E. Asher. Oxford: Heinemann.

Office

It was eight o'clock when he left the office. He felt unbearably tired as he started to walk. The line at the bus stop stretched all the way down the sidewalk. He got in line. There was only one bus that went toward where he lived. Number thirty-two. And on it, shopkeepers galore. When the shops closed at seven-thirty, they poured out from Karol Bagh and Connaught Place.

He couldn't stand to wait very long in the tussle and bustle of the bus stop. Unbearable fatigue. Really unusual. Was this exhaustion from working until eight o'clock without stopping? After all it really wasn't all that unusual for him to work until eight. Standing and standing, his feet ached. Finally, he decided to hail a cab. Just let it end. It was one rupee, eighty paisa from the office to where he lived. And one rupee, ten paisa from the boss's house.

There was no rush at the taxi stand. A few taxis lay there as though they had died. He climbed in one and sat down. As the cab took off, the wind blew inside with a thin hum. Then his eyes wilted and closed. Sleep seized his head. When he arrived at home yesterday, even nocturnal Mallikh from the neighborhood was asleep. Yesterday he worked at the boss's house. Due to a small illness he did not come to the office . . . he didn't much feel like paying for a cab. He walked. When he reached his room, he saw Nanu asleep slumped against the wall.

I need to get a good sleep tonight. Then maybe I won't be so exhausted.

He gave the cab-driver some money. The guy didn't return the twenty paisa difference. Instead, he simpered a sinister smile, "No change."

They're all crooks. If that's not change hanging in his uniform shirt pocket, then what is it?

"Ms. Shalini came by," Nanu the servant said when he saw him.

"Well . . . what'd she say?"

"Nothing really. I made her some tea. She drank it and left."

It had been more than two months since he'd been to Shalini's house, he recalled. I'll go today, I'll go tomorrow, he thought. And just like that, days passed. She called him at the office. But he was unable to say even two words to her just then. The boss was standing right next to him. Plus the chaos of work that constricted his breathing. And now the poor girl had stopped by.

Tomorrow he definitely had to go to Shalini's place, he decided.

The servant brought out the plate and put it on the table. A small child. Still, Nanu knew right from wrong. The master just had to wash his hands and approach the table and he would heat up the rice. Someday he could surely be a butler for some V.I.P. "I'm not going into work tomorrow. So, I won't need my early morning tea, all right, Nanu?" he said in between mouthfuls of rice.

"No tea in the morning!" Nanu repeated as though he didn't believe it.

"I need to get some solid sleep. It's a day off for you, too, so go ahead and rest."

Nanu was elated. No need to wake up at the crack of dawn, light the stove, and make some tea. Poor Nanu!

After dinner, he rolled out his mat. The praise songs would sound from the nearby temple in the morning. In the loudspeakers. As though God couldn't hear. The racket would probably wake him from his sleep. He shut all the windows. He drew the curtains. No light and no noise should creep in.

He turned off the light and sprawled out on the mat. What a relief! Surely his fatigue would dissipate if he could rest like this for a while. His eyes started to close. Just then someone knocked on the door. He got up, turned on the light, and opened the door. Just as he suspected, it was his neighbor Mallikh. Didn't this guy have any sense of propriety? Midnights weren't for sleeping, they were for bothering others.

"Were you asleep? I just need the paper from the fifteenth."

"Right now you need it?"

"It'd be a big help if I could have it. There's a report in it on housing loans," said Mallikh without a trace of shame.

He opened the almirah and started poking around for the paper.

"They've got a sanction for eight thousand going. It's the second month . . . if I build a house, I'll give you a room. It's just you and the servant, right? One room is more than enough."

It was the hundredth time Mallikh had said this. Him and his house!

"You were late again tonight, huh? Once you're in the private sector, that's how it is. The clock rings five o'clock and you can't fold up your file and head home," Mallikh started.

He yanked out all the papers from the almirah and plopped them down on the floor. The paper was from ten or fifteen days ago and could be anywhere.

"You off tomorrow?"

"Yeah."

"Why's that? You don't usually have any qualms about religious holidays."

Tomorrow was Guru Nanak's birthday. But his office never closed for a religious leader's birthday. No, his boss had to go up to Dehradoon tomorrow. That's why he gave him the day off. How could he tell that to Mallikh?

"Did you get home early today?"

He asked, trying to think of *something* to say. Mallikh got a big grin on his face.

"I haven't been to the office in two days. I'm taking a French leave."

Mallikh uncovered the paper from the fifteenth, folded it up, tucked it in his waist and asked, "What is it your office really does here again?"

"We only act as representative. But we're always swamped because we're so shorthanded. Bonus, Provident Fund—we don't have any arrangements like that."

"You all are lucky," Mallikh began, "Six percent of our salary gets deposited into the G.P.F. Compulsory. We only see the remainder. And a stenographer makes more in the private sector than one of our officers. It's pointless to join the government service."

Mallikh sighed. Poor guy. His hair had already gone gray. He was still just an old assistant. He earned almost twice what Mallikh made. He utterly delighted in that fact. What good is a bonus or Provident Fund, if one gets a reasonable wage?

Shoving the paper under his arm, Mallikh left. Talking about work made him forget his sleepiness and his exhaustion. That's just the way he was. He shut the door, turned off the light, and lay down. Even then, he couldn't get work off his mind. There was still an enormous amount of work left to do. The start-up plans for the new branch were already under way. He had already paid the advance to lease the building. Within a month or two, work would begin on setting up the new office. A promotion was almost certain for him. He also had his eye on the servants' quarters next to the new office building. It would be great, if he could get it. He could pocket the rent he's paying now for the room. People at his age kill for such a setup. But, still, all that would come with no sleep and no food, and only after he'd worked himself to death. Today he went to the office at eight in the morning and returned at eight at night. He even worked straight through the lunch break.

Contrary to his wish, he woke up very early in the morning. As usual he had shut all the windows and the room was totally dark. Pulling the blanket over his head, he tried to fall asleep again. He just couldn't get back to sleep. It had been a very long time since he'd had a day off. Ah . . . the days when mornings sauntered by and he forgot all about getting up!

In the end, he abandoned his attempt to sleep. He got up and opened the window. A soft yellow sunlight slipped into the room. He waited for his tea. Then he remembered that he'd told the servant that he didn't want morning tea. Damn. Drinking tea just after waking up had become a habit. Besides tea, there was nothing else unnecessary or untoward about his personality. He didn't smoke. He didn't drink. But if he didn't get his tea, it was as though nothing went according to plan.

He went toward the kitchen. Near the threshold to the kitchen, lying there all covered and rolled up, Nanu. Poor guy! Let him sleep, no need to wake him. Taking care not to step on him, he entered the kitchen.

He lit the stove. It was only after his small little recent promotion that he'd hired Nanu to work for him. Until then, he had made himself tea and lunch. He knew how to prepare the basics. Maybe even better than Nanu.

" Wh . . . whwho's there?"

Nanu woke with a jerk as he heard the clanking of pots. Seeing him, Nanu distressedly rolled up the mat he was sleeping on and placed it in the corner.

"What are you doing, sir?" Nanu asked, wiping the sleep from his eyes.

He didn't say a word. For Nanu, it was quite a shock to see him making tea. He wears pants and neckties and goes to the office after all, right? He put the pot down on the table and walked toward the bedroom. Nanu was saved.

Within fifteen minutes, Nanu brought the prepared tea. As he drank it, Nanu asked: "Sir, didn't you say yesterday that you didn't want morning tea today?"

"What am I supposed to do, Nanu? I tried to sleep as long as I could this morning."

"That's how it goes, sir. It's become a habit for you to wake up so early."

He blew on his tea as he drank. Nanu continued: "Why did you light the stove, sir? Why didn't you call me?"

"I didn't want to disturb you."

It seemed as though Nanu didn't understand. He took the emptied glass and left.

When he had finished his tea, he started his morning regimen. He went to the bathroom. He shaved. Right away Nanu filled his bucket with water. He always bathed in fresh water. Even when the mercury hit freezing in January!

Even in those days, there weren't a handful of people who still bathed by hand with fresh water.

Just as the clock struck eight, he finished his regimen, dressed, and took his keys—the only thing left was to go to the office. But today, there was no office. He felt an emptiness. It had been many, many days since he had not gone to the office. He stood looking vacantly toward the street struck by the sunlight just outside the window and thought—I don't have to take leave today. If the boss wanted to go somewhere, let him. Why should he force the rest of us to take leave?

"Good morning!"

Mallikh called out from the road. He was wearing his khadi "closed-neck" coat. He had a yellow hat on his head. He was going on a trip.

"I've gotta to go to Ghaziabad, to the Mrs.' house."

He was shocked. Traveling all morning on a bus and then a rickshaw, going all the way out past the city to Ghaziabad. What a pain in the ass!

"When will you return?" Nanu exclaimed from the kitchen.

"Tonight."

Locking their room, Mrs. Mallikh came outside along with her children. The group hurriedly walked toward the bus stop.

Then he remembered Shalini. Why shouldn't he go to her place? Poor girl. She came all the way here yesterday after all. Shalini's house was at the south end of town. It must be an hour and a half on the bus.

It was better not to think about spending his day off traveling all that way on the bus.

He liked Shalini. She always blinked her eyes very tenderly as though her eyelids carried a burden. The slow grace with which she opened and closed her eyes made listening to her sweet flirtations a pleasure.

He had only been to her place once. He took the bus. He was totally beat by the time he got there. All his enthusiasm drained away. He was meeting her father for the first time. The old man was wearing an old coat over his sweater. Although unnecessary, his head and ears were swathed in a scarf. He was intently reading the study *Who is After Nehru?* In mid-sentence, he asked: "Who is to succeed Nehru in your opinion?"

He didn't like the question. Reason being he was totally uninterested in it. So he made no reply. Mistaking his silence for thoughtful reflection, the old man said: "Forget it . . . it's pointless to make predictions in such cases anyway. Home came after Macmillan! Was it expected?"

He still said nothing. Truth be told, he had no idea when Lord Home had become Sir Alec Douglas-Home. He hadn't been reading the paper lately, even though he bought it. Why should he buy a paper if he's not going to read it? Wasting money for no reason. He thought about canceling the paper.

Butler's situation was pitiful. "At least he became the victim." Even then, he gave no opinion. If they had talked about Christine Keeler, he could have mustered up an opinion. But the old man liked international politics, it seemed. He just couldn't reconcile himself to the old man.

He didn't feel like presenting himself in front of the old man again. He'll see Shalini some other time. If she wanted, maybe he'd go to her office tomorrow. Sitting around the office with no work to do would make him sleepy.

He stood fixed near the window. Time wouldn't pass. He tried reading the paper. He tried cleaning up. Nothing worked. He stood there looking outside. The street, sunk in sunlight, shade trees bowing their heads. The road filled with people. Hadn't Mallikh got the bus yet? He recognized his ratty, disheveled nest of hair from way off.

Totally bored. Time wouldn't pass. It wasn't even nine. What could he do now?

He put on his clothes. Locked his room. Told Nanu he'd be

back in a little while. He set foot on the road and walked. It was only five minutes, if he went by bus. But how long would he have to wait for the bus? Walking would be good. Mild sun, gentle breeze . . .

He arrived in front of a building made of red brick. As he climbed the steps, he heard Narayanan's speech from the inner room. "En France, un repas sans fromage est comme une belle fille avec un oeil." (In France, a meal without cheese is like a beautiful girl with one eye.)

Him and his French!

"Who's that there? Ramakrishnan from Veppinkadu!"

Narayanan said, opening the door. Narayanan took his shoulder and led him inside. On the floor, Hariharan was polishing some shoes. Baby was flipping through a law book.

"How long has it been?" said Hariharan.

"Sit down." Baby brought a chair for him.

"Looks like that's a new shirt?" Narayanan's eyes fixed on his unwrinkled cotton blend shirt with a fitted tie collar.

"It's Aristo, isn't it?"

"Yeah."

"I would have gotten cream."

"We came by your house last Sunday," said Hariharan, "but your servant said you were at the office."

"At the office on Sunday?" Baby said, closing her book *Lawyer.*

He thought back. He had gone to the office last Sunday, too. He was preparing the accounts for a dinner and reception held for a well-known foreign scientist—it was urgent.

"I think your shirt's a little tight in the shoulder," Narayanan offered.

"Shalini's doing well, I hope," Baby inquired. He chuckled.

"Are you gonna be like this even if you get married?"

"Going to the office at the crack of dawn and coming back in the middle of the night. Not even taking Sundays off. She'd divorce you . . . within a week!"

"So what if he went to the office seven days a week? Look

at his shirt and pants. It's good to be able to dress decently," Narayanan interjected.

"We're going to the movies. You wanna come?" Hariharan said, sliding his feet inside his socks.

"It's *The Brothers Karamazov*. I don't know if you'd like it."

"He wouldn't like it. No Brigitte Bardots or Marilyns in it."

"I think I saw *The Brothers Karamazov* three years ago or so. Didn't you read it?"

"I didn't read it," he said.

"It's a good movie. You should come. You don't have anywhere else to go, do you?"

"No, thanks, I'm not coming," he said, declining Hariharan's invitation.

Everyone finished dressing. Locking the door, Baby said, "You should come by more often. We lived together for two years, after all."

The three young people walked off. He stood watching them for a moment. Then he started walking back home.

"Have you made lunch?" he asked as soon as he reached home.

"It's only ten o'clock."

"Make it quickly. I've gotta go."

"Where are you going, sir? To Ms. Shalini's house?"

"Just hurry up with that lunch," he urged.

He walked to the window and stood there. The bustle in the street was increasing. No line at the bus stop. Instead a big, chaotic mass. A crazed rush!

Having finished his lunch, he left the house. He didn't even glance at the bus stop. He went straight for the taxi stand. The cab screeched to a halt in front of his office. The watchman playing cards in the courtyard of the neighboring building came running. The watchman's face paled as though he'd been scared by a cat. He didn't say anything. It was a day off, right? Everyone was enjoying themselves. Why shouldn't he enjoy himself?

The watchman opened the gate for him. The elevator wasn't

working—no operator. So he had to take the stairs. The big building was asleep—after six days of commotion. His office was on the third floor in a corner. He opened the door. Not a peep. A chance to work with total concentration.

Firs, he decided he should send replies to C. S. Goyal and Lal Chandni. He had received Goyal's third letter two days ago. All he wanted to know were a few insignificant details. Even so, he was embarrassed . . .

"There's no branch office in our building. We only act as representative. But I am pleased to inform you that a branch office will open soon. I am appending the names of cities with branch offices and all other relevant details below . . . ." He readied his reply to Goyal.

Lal Chandni needed some technical information. He started checking old files and ledgers to collect the data. As he sat in the silent room happily working, he forgot it all—Shalini, his friends, the crowded roads . . . and not just that—himself.

Parrots

The gentleman took his napkin, wiped his lips, and stood up from his lunch-table. He picked up his cane lying on the chair. Made of sandalwood with a silver handle, his cane was a masterpiece. Bracing himself with his cane, he walked across the carpeted floor. The soles of his feet were tender, shriveled, and twisted. And so he had bought the soft carpet for 5,000 from the Tibet House in Jor Bagh. The clock on the wall rang sweetly. The old clock had been made in England sometime in the middle of the last century. He walked on top of the red carpet. The gown he wore dragged behind him. The blue gown adorned with stitched images was always warm. The gentleman descended the marble steps of his bungalow. He began to breath heavily as he walked toward the garden. Soft sunlight spread over the green, grassy lawn. Flowers danced in the breeze. He headed straight for his easy chair. Behind him dressed in white followed his servant with the newspaper. The gentleman reclined in the chair. He took the paper and opened it. The servant sat down on the grass and rubbed the gentleman's feet.

The gentleman finished reading the paper. With the tip of his hookah in his mouth, he relaxed in the chair. The gentleman's eyes surveyed his surroundings. Gray and wizened were his eyes. His eyes descended from the sky where birds danced and played. They paused on top of the bungalow bathed in sunlight. Then his eyes traveled on. They fixed on the garage. From there they wandered to the servant's quarters, where the parrot's cage caught his eye. Then his eyes traveled on. To the street emptied of vehicles, to the intertwined neem trees . . . the gentleman's eyes returned to the parrot's cage. There was no parrot in the cage. He asked Ramakrishnan, who was rubbing his feet: "Wasn't there a parrot in that cage, Ramakrishnan?"

"Yes, sir," said the servant respectfully.

The gentleman looked carefully. He did not see a parrot. Ramakrishnan also looked. He, too, saw no parrot in the cage. The gentleman got up from his chair. Ramakrishnan, too, got up. The gentleman headed for the parrot's cage. Behind him, Ramakrishnan also walked. The gentleman stopped in front of the cage. The parrot was lying dead to one side of the cage. Its eyes were half-closed. Its legs were stiff. The parrot had died.

"Ramakrishnan," the gentleman said, "how did the parrot die?"

"Don't know," the servant gently informed him.

"Did it have some illness? Weren't you feeding it regularly?"

"It had no illness, sir," Ramakrishnan explained, "It often tried to dismantle the cage and jump out. It would peck and pull at the trellis work. It would make a racket flapping its wings and such. But that was only for a few days. After that the parrot stopped moving. It stopped making noise. It didn't eat. It didn't drink. All day long it would just sit there paralyzed."

The gentleman looked once more at the parrot. A half-torn bill, half-opened eyes.

"What are you going to do with the parrot, Ramakrishnan?" he asked.

"Shall I give it to Hernandez's cat? Hernandez the driver?"

"Bury it," ordered the gentleman. Ramakrishnan opened the cage; he took out the parrot, dug a hole in the ground, and buried the parrot in the warm earth.

The gentleman returned to the garden. He sat in the easy chair. He took the end of the hookah and put it in his mouth. The servant began to rub his feet.

"Enough," he declared. The servant stood and went away.

He didn't feel like smoking his hookah. He put the end of it down and opened the paper. He couldn't read. He folded the paper back up. He closed his eyes and lay back in his chair. Then he remembered a parrot's cage hanging at a place in Sundara Nagar market. In it sat a parrot who was usually asleep. He stood up. He walked to the garage. Hernandez was sleeping in a corner of the shed. The gentleman opened the car door. He climbed in and drove the car out. Hernandez jumped up, but the gentleman drove the car straight to the market. He saw the parrot's cage hanging in front of the candy shop. He stopped the car and leaped out.

"Will you give me this parrot?"

The parrot belonged to the paan vendor. The shopkeeper looked at the gentleman's face suspiciously.

"I'll give you five rupees. Please give me the parrot." The gentleman held out a five-rupee note. The shopkeeper hesitantly accepted the money. He held out the parrot and cage in return. The gentleman took the cage and opened it. He took the parrot in his hands and threw it upwards. With a joyous sound, the parrot flew off. As it flew higher and higher, the gentleman's eyes sparkled. Did they also tear up?

"Where else can I get a parrot?" he asked.

The shopkeeper thought for a moment.

"In Jangpuram or in Naizamuddin you'll surely get one."

The gentleman walked back to his car. He drove toward Naizamuddin. Pattamars going to Faridabad, buses, diplomats' Cadillacs, Madams on horseback out to feel the breeze. He turned down a narrow lane. Buildings running by. Men defecating in the drainage ditches. Men, women, babies, old people. A crumbling cemetery, a coir mattress in its shadow. An old Muslim with a white cap lying in it. Smoking a hookah. He stopped the car. He got out with determination.

"Does anyone raise parrots here?" he asked the old man.

The old man stroked his beard.

"Yes, in A Block, in Mr. Ram Kumar Luggani's house."

The gentleman thanked him and got back in his car. He

inquired at A Block and found Luggani's house. A sturdy bungalow, a car in the garage, dogs at the gate. The gentleman got out of his car. He walked to the bungalow, his gown dragging on the ground. Beads of sweat ran down his regal countenance. The dogs didn't bark. They moved aside out of respect. Luggani, who was sitting in the flower garden, stood up and came out.

"Do you keep a parrot?"

He followed Luggani inside. Luggani showed him. A huge golden cage. A cage and a green parrot. Before it was a banana and milk, but the parrot was uneasy.

"Will you give me the parrot, sir?"

"I guard this parrot as though it were gold."

"Please, sir, kindly give it to me."

Luggani looked at the gentleman's gown, his cane, his car. He called his servant, "Take the parrot's cage and give it to this gentleman."

The servant took the cage.

"Shall I put it in the car?"

"Give it here, please."

The gentleman pulled away the cage. He opened it and took the parrot in his hands. He lifted both his hands and released it upwards. The parrot flew up toward the blue sky. The gentleman watched the parrot until it disappeared from his sight. He took Luggani by the hand and calmly said: "Many thanks."

The gentleman walked to his car. Streams of perspiration now flowed down his temples. He drove. Narrow lanes. Congested shops on both sides. Pigs in the drainage ditches. Magicians in the street, prostitutes behind purdahs in the bustling buildings. Jangpuram. He stopped the car. A butchery stood close by. He approached the red-bearded butcher.

"I want some parrots."

"Parrots?"

"Where can I get some?"

"Is one enough?"

The gentleman shook his head yes.

"Kaseem," the butcher called.

A boy named Kaseem came.

"Show this gentleman to Abdulla Mirsai's house."

Kaseem walked. The gentleman followed behind. They entered a narrow street. Wash water flowed along the ground. The end of the gentleman's gown snaked in the mud. Kaseem walked. They crossed several zigzagging streets. The gentleman was winded. He hobbled along with the cane in his hand. They stopped in front of a burial tomb that had been converted into a house.

"Abdulla's house."

Kaseem turned to walk away. The gentleman reached in the pocket of his gown and gave him a rupee. Taking out another large bill, he entered the burial tomb. A parrot's cage was hanging inside. An old man sat dyeing his beard with henna.

"Please give me this parrot," said the gentleman pointing to the parrot's cage. He took the bill and put it in the old man's hand. The old man took down the cage and gave it to him. The gentleman opened the cage and with both hands grabbed the parrot and sent it flying up. The parrot soared above. Several minutes later, the gentleman arrived back at the street. Just before getting in his car, he asked the butcher:

"I want a bunch of parrots. Do you know where I can get some?"

"Try Sardar Bazaar or Chandni Chowk," the old man said. The gentleman got in the car. He dropped it off a mile or so later at Chandni Chowk.

The sun was piercingly hot. The road tar softened. The horses carrying loads panted and wheezed from fatigue. The pigs snorted around looking for shade. People emptied the streets. He stopped the car outside the old garden called Chandni Chowk. The gentleman had worn himself out inquiring about parrots. When he saw a parrot shop in front of the Motti Theater, his eyes lit up. Tiny shop, thick with cages. And in the cages, parrots without number.

"How much for a parrot?"

"Three rupees for one; eight rupees for three."

"How much for all your parrots?"

The man counted the parrots. There were over a hundred.

The gentleman put his hand in his pocket. Only a few one-rupee notes. He went to his car and wrote out a check.

As the parrots' owner stood by wide eyed, the gentleman freed the parrots one by one. He took the parrots in his hand and threw them upwards. Opening cage after cage the bars pricked his hands causing them to bleed. Scores of parrots given their freedom flew and played above Chandni Chowk. Out of breath, hands bleeding, the gentleman continued his exhausting march. Asking about parrots. To Daryaganj, to the Ajmeeri Gate, to Sabzimandi he trudged. The sun set. Darkness fell. Searching for his car somewhere near a bridge, he walked. Blood stains covered his gown. He only had one shoe left. He was panting like a horse as he walked. His legs wobbled. He found his car at the base of an unlit lamppost. The gentleman opened the door and fell inside. He rested his face on the steering wheel. Darkness enveloped the car. With a slight heave he vomited blood. The gentleman fell dead in the car.

The innumerable parrots that the gentleman had freed flew and played above the city in the light of the stars.

Radha, Just Radha

When Radha left campus and started walking home, she saw Suresh standing at the bus stop. She was delighted to see him. They had spent an hour yesterday evening walking along the beach, on the sands strewn with seashells, in the salty whispers of the wind. She never expected to run into him again so soon. She cut across the street and walked toward him. Suresh was smoking a cigarette, staring off into the distance somewhere. It made her smile to think how glad he would be at the unplanned surprise of seeing her. Though she stopped right in front of him, he continued to stare off into space. He did not even notice her. She moved a little closer to him. Their shoulders touched. Releasing his mouthful of smoke he looked directly at her. Then he moved over a little and took another drag of his cigarette. There was not even a hint of surprise or joy on his face when he saw her.

"Suresh!"

Again he turned and looked at her.

"Suresh, where are you going?"

He looked at her as though he did not understand. She pulled out a magazine from among the books pressed against her chest and said, "Look at this. 'Ping' is inside." She opened the magazine, found the page where Samuel Beckett's poem was printed, and held it out to him. He looked back and forth from her face to the magazine.

"You read it first. Then I'll read it," she said, holding the magazine out to him.

He dropped his dying cigarette on the street and put it out with his shoe. Then he asked, "Who are you, girl?"

She burst out laughing when she heard him. She forgot they were at the bus stop where a crowd of people was standing. Still holding out the magazine, she said, "You go ahead and take this now. You can bring it with you when you come to my house Saturday."

"Saturday? Whose house?"

"Dinner at my house Saturday night? Ring a bell?"

"I have no idea what you are talking about . . . "

"All right, enough kidding around."

The smile on her face, the smile that never went out, vanished. He turned to face her squarely and said in a serious tone, "Listen, are you playing around with me, or what? I've never seen you before in my life . . . "

She did not understand what he was saying. And his behavior upset her.

"It's not me who's playing around. It's you." Her face became dour.

"You must be mistaking me for someone else. I'm *not* the person you're looking for."

"Suresh. Aren't you Suresh? Don't you think I know who I'm talking to?"

"I'm Suresh all right, but I don't know you."

"Oh, you don't know me? You don't know Radha?"

"No."

His voice deepened. Taking out another cigarette, he lit up and exhaled the smoke.

"Two days ago, didn't you come to my college and ask for me? And yesterday, didn't we go to the beach together?"

"No, I did *not* go to any college to see anyone. And I did not go to the beach with anyone either."

Her face blanched.

"Please go away," he said, "Can't you see everyone staring?"

He moved away from her. The bus arrived. Suresh threw down his cigarette and got on the bus. The bus drove off through the crowded street and disappeared around the corner. She slid the magazine back in between her books and walked off, her head bowed. Everything will be okay, if I can just get home, she thought.

When the main road ended, she walked along the path of red earth toward her house. She passed by Bhaskaran's tea shop on the way. Bhaskaran lifted his head from his tea and looked at her. He asked Kannan Master, who was waiting for his tea, "Who's that girl walking by?"

Master shrugged and fanned out his fingers.

Her house was just around the corner from Bhaskaran's shop. As usual, her father had come home from the office and was sitting on the front porch in his easy chair reading the paper. When she entered the courtyard, her father lifted his head from the page, adjusted his glasses, and looked straight at her. Her bowed head ascended the verandah.

"Yes . . . who are you, please?" her father said taking his glasses in hand, "I'm afraid I don't know you . . . "

Her chest heaved when she heard him. She froze in midstep.

"Where are you from? Have a seat . . . Madhavi!"

"Daddy!"

Her voice quivered.

"Daddy?"

Her father stood up from his chair and pulled up his loosened dhoti as he walked toward her.

"Who are you, dear? Where are you from?"

Unable to say anything, she stood there staring at her father's face in utter confusion.

"Madhavi! . . . Madhavi!"

Her father went to the doorway. He stuck his head inside and bellowed for her mother. Her mother chirped quickly from somewhere inside. A couple of minutes later, after finishing her bath and changing her clothes, her mother came out with a red dot of sandal paste on her forehead.

Her father approached her mother and said in a hushed voice, "Some girl? She doesn't answer when I talk to her. Something must have happened. I don't know . . . "

"She didn't say where she was from?"

"Doesn't she have to tell me? If she's not speaking, how am I supposed to know?!"

Her mother looked at her from head to toe and said, "It seems she's from a good family. Poor girl."

"Dear . . . here. Sit here," her father said as he offered her a chair. She continued to stand there like a statue.

Her mother came over and touched her shoulder, saying, "Please sit, dear."

Her mother took her and sat her down in the chair. The hands that held her books were trembling.

"What's your name, dear? Where are you from?"

"Mommy!"

"Please tell us what your trouble is. We'll do whatever we can to help you. Won't we, Madhavi?" her father said looking to her mother.

The books in her hands slipped and fell to the floor. They scattered on the floor around her feet.

"Why are you saying this to me, Daddy? I don't understand . . . "

"Daddy?"

Her father looked at her with surprise.

"Am I your father?"

"Why are you tormenting me like this? I can't stand it!"

"Who's tormenting you, dear?" There was compassion in her mother's voice.

"Mommy, Daddy, don't you know me? What's happened to you . . . to everyone?! I can't bear it . . . I can't!"

Her eyes filled with tears. Her mother and father stood there watching her, not understanding at all. She stood up from the chair and started to walk inside. She felt like running to her room upstairs and crying face down into her pillow. As she put her foot inside, her mother came forward and stopped her:

"Where are you going?"

"To my room. I want to lie down . . . I can't bear this!"

"Your room?"

To her father, "I think something's wrong with her mind."

"We're just going around in circles here . . . " her father said, wrenching his hands.

"You're the ones who are sick in the head. How can a mother and father not know their own daughter when they see her?!"

Her face reddened with tears.

"You are not our daughter."

Amidst the tears and sobs, she said, "I'm Radha. Don't you know Radha when you see her?"

"You are not Radha."

"I *am* Radha . . . Radha."

"No . . . no . . . "

"Mommy, haven't you cooked rice for me these past eighteen years? How can you say such things?"

Her mother said nothing but looked at her with sorrow and sympathy.

"Daddy, wasn't it you who performed my writing ceremony? Wasn't it you who sacrificed your own sleep to help me with my math at exam time? Wasn't it you who took me to the movies last Sunday? How could you forget all of this?"

He touched her shoulders and said with a smile, "Excellent! What wonderful fairy tales you tell!"

"Fairy tales?!"

Her viscous tears erased her mother and father standing before her.

Her father returned to his chair and placed his glasses on his nose.

"Please tell us where you are from and what you want. We'll do what we can for you. Enough of the games."

"It's already sunset. I think you should stay here tonight and then tomorrow you can go wherever you want to go."

"Where am I supposed to go? This is my home!"

"This is not your home."

"Madhavi, don't say any more. It's only because her mind is unstable that she's saying all of this . . . "

"If you don't want to stay here tonight, then you should get going. If you need to be somewhere before dark, go ahead and go," her mother said.

Her father returned to reading his paper.

"Where will I go, Mommy? I have no one except you and Daddy . . . "

She could not continue. Misery clutched her throat. She stood crying on the porch for several minutes. Her father did not take his eyes off the newspaper. Her mother leaned quietly against the wall. Empty distress crept across her mother's paled face. Realizing this, she wiped her eyes with her palms. Her quivering legs slowly stepped down; she exited the courtyard; she stepped out onto the street; she walked away. Oil lamps burned in the windows of the houses along the street. Children reciting the names of gods stopped to give her the glance of unfamiliarity. Birds returning to their nests looked down on the stranger. Trees swayed in the whistling ocean gusts. The sea crashed against the shore. Darkness poured across the sky and the land, filling them. The birds, the trees, the ocean gusts, the sky, the land—in a single voice, they sang:

"You are not Radha. We know you not."

Bathroom

Purushottaman has a wish.

O Bhagavati of Korom, please make Purushottaman's wish come true—

Guruvayurappa, please fulfill Purushottaman's wish—

Lord Ayyappa, please bring Purushottaman's wish to fruition—

He never wishes for anything. The poor fool. Even as a child, he never wished for anything. Merchants from distant places used to sell whistles, balloons, balls, and such at the Thira Festival in Korom.

Purushottaman never demanded anything.

"Mommy, get me a balloon. A red balloon."

He never demanded.

"Daddy, get me a ball."

Never.

"Mommy, get me a whistle."

Even when he grew up, Purushottaman never had a desire.

He didn't want a terrycloth shirt.

He didn't want a watch.

He didn't want money for the movies.

Purushottaman is a man who has never desired anything. Well, now this same Purushottaman has a desire—he wants to be a housefly.

O Bhagavati of Korom, please make Purushottaman a housefly—

Guruvayurappa, please make him a housefly—

Lord Ayyappa, please make Purushottaman a housefly—

Most High and Benevolent God. If you could please fulfill Purushottaman's humble desire—

Purushottaman wants to be a housefly.

Everyone has a wish. One person wants to win the lottery. Another wants a beautiful wife. Others want children. Some people long to find a job.

And the just Lord grants their various wishes. If he didn't, how, in his whole life, could Madhavan the horse-cart driver hope to have such great luck?

Madhavan bought the one-rupee lottery ticket from Abubakkar's luggage shop. He tucked it in his waist. As he walked to his shack, he prayed, "God, let me win the lottery this time!"

Would the Most High and Benevolent God refuse to make Madhavan's wish come true? Or allow only Madhavan's wish to come true? Buck-toothed Bhaskaran had also made a wish, "I wish I had a beautiful wife."

By the time Bhaskaran's desire reached his mind, God had already sent a beautiful wife his way. A beauty with lots of hair and pearls for teeth.

Gopalan Master wished, "If only I had a son . . . "

When Gopalan Master's wife delivered, it was a baby boy. Would the God who so graciously blessed Madhavan, Bhaskaran, and Gopalan Master fail to bless Purushottaman?

Purushottaman has a wish.

Purushottaman wants to be a housefly.

The desire to be a housefly crept into Purushottaman's mind yesterday. Just yesterday. Nevertheless, he suffers as if it's been a thousand years. The fire of his desire crackles hot and bright.

"Is Vasanta here?"

Lifting his head from the newspaper, Gopalan Master looked through his glasses, "Purushottaman? What's the matter, kid? Sunrise is pretty early for a visit."

Gopalan Master was stretched out in his chair.

"Sit. Dear! Lakshmi! Look who's come for a visit!"

There was no answer from inside.

"She's probably at the well."

Master again populated his chair. Purushottaman stood up and walked inside. He didn't see anyone there. He pulled up his dhoti and tied it. Then, with a little whistle, he proceeded toward the well.

Lakshmi-amma was standing next to the well brushing her teeth.

"What's the matter, my dear?" she said politely.

"Is Vasanta here?"

"She's taking a bath."

Purushottaman noticed only then that the bathroom was closed shut. He could hear the splash and plunge of water being drawn and poured, drawn and poured.

Vasanta was taking a bath.

Purushottaman felt ill for some reason. The smile on his face, that permanent smile, instantly vanished.

Lakshmi-amma was talking and brushing her teeth at the same time.

Purushottaman did not understand what she was saying. Nor did he hear her laugh.

He just stood there staring at the closed door. The only thing his ears heard was the sound of water being drawn and poured, drawn and poured.

The sound of the water stopped. The door opened.

Untied hair. Wet, red glass bangles on her wrists. White drops on her neck and cheeks.

A smile blooming in the wetness!

"Ettan?—"

"He's been waiting for you," Lakshmi-amma reported.

"I'll be right back, okay?"

Vasanta went back inside with her wet towel and soap-dish.

That was when he saw it: in the bathroom filled with the aroma of soap and oil, a housefly was flying around in circles.

The housefly who can see everything.

Purushottaman anguished, envious of the fly.

His heart beat a big drum. His feet quivered. His face paled like paper.

That lucky housefly! That very lucky housefly!

Why was Purushottaman born a man? Forget being born a king—forget being born an emperor—Purushottaman yearned to be born a housefly.

In the bathroom permeated with the scents of medicated oil and soap, lurking along the wall, watching Vasanta . . .

O God, make me a housefly.

Bhagavati, Ayyappa, Guruvayurappa, Mathappumuttappa, hear my prayer. Make me a housefly. I want nothing else in this life. I will never ask for anything else.

Please make me a housefly.

Please make me a housefly.

Can God refuse?

The Most High and Benevolent God created gods specifically for the purpose of fulfilling human desires. A god was born specifically to make Madhavan the horse-cart driver win the lottery. To give buck-toothed Bhaskaran his beautiful wife. A god was born specifically to give Gopalan Master a boy.

And God had to create a god specifically to fulfill Purushottaman's desire. If that god could not fulfill it, God would again create himself. He would recreate himself into another god capable of fulfilling Purushottaman's desire. Another god more powerful than the first.

Purushottaman prayed. He prayed night and day. Please make me a housefly. Please make me a housefly.

He begged the trees and the seedlings, "Dear trees and seedlings, please make me a housefly."

He begged the crakes, "Dear crakes, please make me a housefly."

He begged the animals of the earth, the birds, and the snakes, "Please make me a housefly."

The trees and seedlings called out, "O Lord, make Purushottaman a housefly."

The crakes flew up to the sky with prayers in their beaks, "Most High and Benevolent God, fulfill Purushottaman's wish."

"Make Purushottaman a housefly," the animals howled to God.

"Make Purushottaman a housefly," the birds sang to God.

"Make Purushottaman a housefly," the snakes hissed to God.

"Make Purushottaman a housefly," the insects buzzed.

God opened his eyes and smiled.

Thin, fibrous legs attached to his belly—on tiny little wings—Purushottaman flew toward Vasanta's house.

As usual, Gopalan Master was sitting in his easy chair reading his paper. Master didn't see Purushottaman fly by with a whistle.

Purushottaman exited the house through the back door and flew toward the bathroom.

Inside the bathroom, he stuck himself against the wall. From here, he could see everything. Everything.

With a palpitating heart, eyes wide open, he awaited Vasanta's arrival. Seconds, seconds that lasted eons. Or eons like seconds that splintered and tumbled down in the bathroom.

Someone's footsteps. Are they Vasanta's? O Lord, let it be Vasanta. I can't bear to wait any longer . . . I simply can't . . .

I'll die if I don't . . .

Vasanta entered, soap dish and towel in hand. The glass bangles on her wrists chimed as she unbanded her hair.

She fastened the lock on the door.

She poured the medicated oil in her hands and rubbed it into her hair. Thick hair, black like eyeliner, rolling down to her waist.

Accompanied by the music of the bangles, she undid the buttons on her blouse . . .

Purushottaman saw nothing. Heard nothing. He had gone mad.

Purushottaman did not see the house lizard prowling, creeping quietly toward him from the other corner of the wall.

And he did not know it was the house lizard who devoured him.

Tea

Dad's getting old. His hair's gone all white. Gray stubble covers his face now that he's stopped shaving. It gives his face a sort of miserable look. He always speaks in a soft and pained voice.

Every day around noon Dad has the habit of taking a long nap. In an ornately carved bed that is as old as he is, Dad sleeps on one side, his eyes only half closed. He doesn't even wake up when the children return from school making a ruckus in the late afternoon. So, finally, Mother crept toward him and gently called out, "It's five o'cloooock."

Although Dad woke up instantly, he still lay there without opening his eyes. Then lit a cheroot. Slowly blowing out the smoke, he said, "I just completely fell asleep. My body just doesn't feel right."

"Shall I bring you some tea?" Mother asked.

"Um."

"Nalini," Mother called out, "bring some tea for your father."

Nalini brought the tea in a small glass. She was a long-eyed young girl with a flushed face from constantly working in the kitchen. Her clothes were smudged and smeared. "The tea's very hot," she said.

When the tea cooled bit, Mother took the glass to the bedside. Eyes closed, smoking his cheroot, Dad said, "Just put it there, I'll drink it later."

Mother leaned against the door and stared at Dad's face. As he sat there, eyes closed, smoking away, his face sank further into depression. Every so often he let out a sigh.

Even after his finishing his smoke, he didn't bother to get out of bed. Mother reminded him, "Isn't your tea getting cold?"

Dad stood up from the bed and fixed his loosened dhoti. Mother brought him the tea. He took a sip and placed it on the table. Mother asked, "What is it?"

"Nothing."

"Not enough sugar?"

"It's fine."

"Then why won't you drink it?" Mother asked as she stared at the tea. "Is it too strong?"

Dad gave no reply. He pushed the window-curtain aside and stared outside. A delicate drizzle of rain shimmered on the empty street.

Mother tasted the tea with a spoon and winced. "Nalini!" she yelled.

Nalini rushed from the kitchen, drying her wet hands in her skirt as she came. Mother asked, "Didn't you put any sugar in this?"

She thought a moment. When she realized her mistake, she bowed her head. Beads of sweat gathered on her face. Mother said, "My God, how absentminded you are!"

Mother went to the kitchen, added some sugar, and returned with the tea. Then she asked, "The tea's gotten a little cold. Shall I warm it up for you?"

"Don't bother." Dad said, continuing to stare out through the window.

"Then have a little, won't you?"

"Didn't I say I'd drink it?" Dad flicked the ashes from the end of his cheroot onto the floor.

The now sweetened, slowly cooling tea sat there on top of the table. Dad relit his cheroot and stood at the window, just looking outside. No matter how much others insisted, he gave no regard to drinking the tea. At the persistent pushing, Dad shouted, "Why do you insist on bothering me? When I feel like drinking it, I will."

"Why are you being so stubborn? It's because she forgot to add the sugar, isn't it?" Mother said worriedly.

Dad didn't say a word. Mother took the tea in her hands and said, "Aren't you going to drink this?"

Without looking at the tea, Dad turned his face away and said, "Well, she did forget, didn't she? How can you all forget such a thing? It just shows how much attention you all really pay to me around here." Dad released the smoke from his cheroot through his nostrils. As Mother stood there speechless, Dad continued, "I told you hundred times that I ran out of cheroots. But did you go and buy me any? When the doctor came this morning, didn't you give me a smelly old dhoti to wear? This is what gets forgotten. Believe me, I understand what's going on."

"I didn't think that the doctor would just suddenly show up like that. As soon as he arrived, I just thought I better get you a dhoti to wear. Do you think I would knowingly do such a thing?" Mother said with her head drooped low.

"You knew exactly what you were doing. If I walk around in a dirty, wrinkled dhoti, what's it to you, right? If I don't get any proper tea or cheroots to smoke, well that's just good for you."

"Don't talk like that." Mother's eyes wetted. Her slowly graying hair had fallen over her face. But in the end those eyes, accustomed as they were to suppressing intense sorrow inside, only caused one to think of a tear, the tear itself never came.

Mother bound back her fallen hair and looked out the window. Her son was approaching along the rain-soaked street with a bunch of papers in hand. Leaning, like Dad, to one side, Mother watched her son walking as though he had something special to share. Mother said, "Ravi's coming."

Ravi stashed the papers on the table and wiped the sweat from his brow as he entered. "Mother, some tea, please," he yelled. He went into Dad's room and gave him a package, "Your cheroots."

Every day when he came home from work, Ravi would bring

his Dad cheroots. This time it was two bundles of cheroots covered in a white wrapper. Untying the bundles, Dad looked at the label and then declared dramatically, "How many days have I been telling that I don't like this brand of cheroot? When I smoke these, it feels like my throat's going to rip. Aren't there any other cheroots to be had in the whole state?"

The happy look on his son's face instantly disappeared. He stammered out a reply, "I don't remember you telling me to buy another brand of cheroot. Did you?"

"No, I didn't tell you to," Dad said diverting his eyes away from his son, "If it saves you two seventy-five to get these, then just bring me this brand. I'll just cough and cough until I die. But at least you'll be spared any inconvenience."

"Dad, if you don't want these cheroots, I'll go back out right now and get you some others."

As though he hadn't heard this, Dad said, "Doesn't anyone around here have the time to listen to what I say? If not, then what's the point of everybody asking how I'm doing, am I comfortable, and all that? I know very well what you all really think about me." Dad's voice was an attack. His sunken eyes fixed on the floor as he complained to no one in particular, "Well, can I get Your Highnesses' permission to take a nap, if I want? I can at least forget everything when my eyes are closed. But as soon as I do, someone comes in to wake me up."

Mother said to her son, "It was after five o'clock when I woke him. I mean, his tea was getting cold. What was I supposed to do? Everything is my fault." Mother sighed and sobbed.

Dad replied, "No, no, of course, you couldn't have done anything wrong. I guess not washing my dirty shirts and bringing me tea without sugar is my fault somehow."

"Say whatever you want. I'll put up with it as always. It's all my fate anyway. It's not like all this started today or yesterday. Have you ever allowed me even one little desire, one indulgence?" Her eyes suddenly teared up.

"So now you're making speeches!?" Dad said, tossing his

spent cheroot on the floor. Mother said nothing. She stood there staring at the floor as though she'd accidentally said something that shouldn't be said. Her expression just encouraged Dad. He continued, "You're standing right here in front of me making a speech, aren't you! That's how much I'm worth to you all. Lecturing me, me who has spent his entire life toiling, wearing out arm and leg for you. You haven't learned a damn thing. Just think about that."

His son said, "Mother will bring you another glass of tea. I'll go get the brand of cheroots you like and then what can you be angry about?"

As he tried to leave, Dad stopped him, "Where do you think you're going? I don't want your cheroots, and I don't want your tea. I'm not begging you for anything. I'm getting old. I can't be as active as I used to. This is what your father has become. Are you even aware of that? You have to buy me cheroots with this in mind. You have to pay attention to your father. Because if you don't, boy, don't expect me to beg and plead. Never. If that day ever comes, then don't expect to see any father around here anymore . . . " Dad's voice faltered.

"Dad, why are you saying all of this? We haven't done anything to you. And even if we had, don't we deserve forgiveness?"

"I forgive you, son. I forgive you. I raised you all. Today you have conjee to eat and a house to sleep in. I shed blood and tears to give you all of this. And in the end, your only desire is to starve and kill me in my old age. And as I tell you all of this, I should forgive you, right?"

His son approached and, calming his voice, said, "Dad, I've noticed the changes happening to you. Tell me what's on your mind. We're all trying every day to make you happy."

Dad looked for a moment at his face. He stood up and said gently, "So, you haven't forgotten this old man, eh?" Dad laughed. "Listen here, boy, don't try your tricks on me. Is it that you think I don't notice what you're thinking, what you're doing around here? Not on your life. So long as there's strength in this tongue, I will speak up for number one. And I will not permit all your dirty schemes, understand?"

His son said, "What tricks are we playing on you? I'd like to know, just tell us. I really think you've just misunderstood a lot of things."

"Right, I misunderstand. There's no truth in anything I say. And right after that comes I've lost my senses, I'm crazy. That's what you'll say."

His son said nothing. Mother's wizened cheeks became wet with tears. Stroking his gray whiskers, Dad continued, "You want to see me as a nut, so you can kick me around like an old dog. And when the neighbors ask, you'll say, 'Dad's gone mad.' What a deceitful trick!"

Mother sobbed into her open hands. When he heard her sobbing, Dad lifted his head. "Why are you crying?" Dad said, looking into Mother's overflowing eyes, "Neither your tears nor your son's demands will shake me. Did you think that I'd be a good dog and wag my tail just because you say so? This is *my* house. The house I sweated and worked for. Whoever lives here has to do what I say. Don't you dare sit here and lecture me!"

Mother said nothing and simply fixed her strained eyes on the floor. His son, too, said nothing—his patience and good grace totally exhausted. His son rubbed his face in exasperation. Staring at him, Dad said, "Why aren't you saying anything? Probably thinking about how it is that you might get rid of this old man and toss him aside. Don't think about it, boy. I'm staying right here in this house. Until I die, understand?"

"Got it," his son said, infuriated. "Dad, you see Mother crying? Do you savor the taste of her tears? Is it that you don't want us to have our own lives even for one day? What do you want? To drive away your wife and children and live here all alone? If that's what you want, just say the word."

His son wrung his hands in disgust and suddenly left the room. He hurtled down the steps and walked through the darkened street deliberately leaning to one side. Dad set his half-smoked cheroot on the windowsill and walked to the verandah, stroking the stubble on his chin.

For a long time Dad leaned in reflection on the pillar and then gently returned to his chair. He reclined a bit and lit a new cheroot, staring blankly at the moistened wick of the lamp. The rain was gathering strength. The water suddenly pelted the courtyard. It formed large bubbles that for a moment shone forth, then burst.

His son returned during a break in the downpour. His clothes were soaking wet. Drops of rain trickled from his hair. Dad was still sitting in his chair. Mother sat on her haunches, her hands on her face. Their son went inside head down, as though he saw neither of them.

Mother looked at the chair and asked in a subdued voice, "Shall I make dinner?"

"Um." Even then Dad sat there smoking away.

When her son came back from changing his wet clothes, Mother was putting dinner on the table. In between serving up heaps of rice on the plates, she wiped the tears from her eyes with the end of her apron. Her son looked at the serving dish and said, "Why are you crying, Mother?"

Mother didn't reply and simply dabbed her eyes again with the corner of her apron. Her face was pale like that of some-one who's ill. When she finished serving the rice, she approached Dad's chair and softly whispered, "Why are you sitting out here in the cold? I have rolled out your bed for you. Have a little supper and then lie down inside, okay? Forgive us for everything that happened."

"I'm not hungry."

"But you barely had anything for lunch. And you didn't even drink your tea."

"I don't want any dinner," Dad said, "Did Ravi eat? If not, tell him to go ahead."

Ravi was sitting in front of the stack of papers he'd brought home from the office.

Mother said, "He won't eat without you. He's waiting for you."

"Ravi!" Dad called. Ravi came to the doorway. Dad said, "You go ahead and eat. Don't wait for me. This is my fate.

What can I do about it?"

Ravi stayed silent, but Dad stared at him and continued, "What are you waiting for? The rice will get cold. Go on."

"You don't want anything, Dad?"

"Didn't I just tell you not to wait for me? I will eat when I'm good and ready. You eat."

Ravi and Mother didn't go to eat dinner. The rain continued to fall. A cold wind. Lightening in the corner of the sky. The wind blew the raindrops inside the verandah. Dad said, "The wind and rain are picking up. You two go and eat something. Close the door and relax."

"Are you trying to get sick, sitting out here fasting in the rain and wind? Why do you insist on worrying and troubling others?"

"Why do you insist on troubling me?" Dad asked. "I'm used to sitting in the rain and hot sun. I won't get sick. And even if I did, why would that trouble anyone?"

"If you don't want to eat anything, that's fine, but at least come in and lie down," Mother said looking in his eyes.

"No matter what I say, you really are dead set on not doing as I ask," Dad said, turning his face away. "I can skip a meal. I can survive the rain and wind. But if you would only do as I say . . . ."

Mother replied, "Have we not done what you've asked somehow?"

"Then go inside, dowse the lamplight, and relax. Don't think about me anymore; such is my fate. I won't be a burden on you much longer. At the most five or six more months, that's all. I still have to have congee and cheroots, but it's only five or six months. If I haven't died by then, I'll find some way not to bother anyone again." Dad's voice choked up.

"The rice is getting cold, Mother," her son said softly from the doorway. Hearing this, Dad got up from his chair and said, "Okay, are you going to stop all this stubbornness? Close the door, and relax inside. Otherwise . . . ."

Dad straightened his loosened dhoti and then added, "Do

what I say, if you know what's good for you. Or else I'll go walking around in this rain. But you'd like that, wouldn't you, if I exposed myself to the cold on top of my fast. You'd love to watch me die like a dog in the middle of the street."

The door creaked shut, the lamp went out. In the dark, pelted by the wind and rain, Dad sat back in his chair and tapped his shirt pocket. No more cheroots. He stooped over and picked through the discarded butts until he found one only half used. He struggled but finally got it lit and took the smoke inside.

Five-and-a-Half-Year Old

Jayan is the only son of Sekharan and Nalini. He is in the first grade.

One school day.

"It's already eight. Isn't Jayan up yet?" Nalini called out from the kitchen as she warmed up the milk. The question was addressed to Sekharan, who was reading the paper on the verandah.

He had to be at the office by ten-thirty. So he woke up at seven-thirty, drank a cup of black coffee, and was now reading the paper.

Jayan had to be at school by nine.

"Please, why don't you just call him?"

"The milk's about ready to boil," Nalini called out again from the kitchen. She was stirring the milk intermittently with a ladle.

After she set out the vessel of milk, she went out to the porch.

"Haven't you woken him up yet? It's past eight o'clock, my God—"

"Krishnamurti is gone, too," said Sekharan to no one at all, his head buried in the paper. Hearing the news, Nalini was confused.

"Krishnamurti? Which Krishnamurti?"

"The one from Sri Kakulam—" he lifted his head from the page, "He was murdered like a dog."

She took the paper away from him.

"It's after eight, and he's just sleeping away like a dumb ox. This is your fault."

"My fault?"

Yesterday, Jayan went to sleep after midnight.

"Do you want another story?" Sekharan asked again when he had finished reading *Cinderella*.

"Yes."

Jayan grabbed his father's big nose and pulled it.

"The one about the lion and the hare?"

"You already told that one—"

"What about the one about the fox who lost his tail?"

"Yeah, that one."

The boy lay there eagerly awaiting the story. His father began.

From *Cinderella* to the story of the fox who lost his tail. From the story of the fox to the story of the wolf and the billy goats. And so it was, past midnight.

"You didn't even care that there was a woman sleeping right next to you."

Nalini felt slighted.

Jayan was the first one to sleep. He slept thinking about Cinderella and the tailless fox and the . . . He lay there sleeping with a smile and a dream on his lips, on his tender lips.

So did Sekharan.

"You know, you get more beautiful every day," said Sekharan as he looked into her eyes. The beautiful woman who stood before him woke up very early that morning, bathed, put sandal on her forehead, and painted her eyes with eyeliner.

"All right, I'll go wake him up," she said, walking inside.

Jayan wasn't asleep. He was lying down, staring at the ceiling, thinking about something.

"Are you up? I thought you were sleeping." She was surprised to find him lying there awake. Usually he ran downstairs as soon as he woke up. Usually he was not the kind of boy to sit or lie still in one place for very long. What was he lying there wondering about today?

"What are you thinking about, baby?" Nalini kissed Jayan on the forehead.

"Probably about that fox who lost his tail," Sekharan answered as he came in.

"It's time to cut your hair, baby." Nalini pushed back Jayan's hair, which was strewn across his forehead.

"We'll do it Sunday—I've gotta get my hair cut, too." Sekharan ran his fingers through his own mop of hair.

"Get up, baby—"

Nalini plucked Jayan up from the bed. He held his head crookedly as though he didn't want to do anything.

"Are you feeling okay, Jayan?"

"He probably didn't get enough sleep," his mother and father commented.

"Hurry up and brush your teeth, and I'll get you a glass of water to drink."

Without saying anything, Jayan got down from the bed, picked up his twig-toothbrush, and went to the side of the well.

Nalini got a glass of water from the bathroom and came outside. "Haven't you brushed your teeth yet?" she asked. Jayan was standing there staring off somewhere, thinking of something.

He brushed his teeth.

"Today, Mommy's gonna help you shower, okay? There's not enough time for you to wash up by yourself."

Jayan didn't fuss at all. He hated other people washing him. But . . .

Nalini washed and dried him, then wrapped a towel around his waist. "Hurry, run and put shirt on," she told him.

She went to the kitchen. She poured some milk in a glass, added some sugar, and stirred it with a spoon.

Jayan came down after changing his clothes.

"Good boy."

She pressed her lips against his oiled hair. Jayan always got lots of kisses from his mother and father, always.

As Jayan was eating breakfast, Nalini set out his book and slate for him.

"Mrs. Nalini, is Jayan ready?" Vatsala called out from the street. She was a little girl, ten or twelve years old, who lived in the neighborhood. Every day Jayan went to and from school with Vatsala.

Nalini grabbed the book and slate, took Jayan by the hand, and went out to the street.

"I'm gonna bring you home some chocolate tonight, son," Sekharan shouted out from the porch.

"I don't think my baby's feeling well today," Nalini said to herself as she handed Jayan his book and slate and watched him walk away with his head bowed.

"Here, let me carry your book and slate for you." Jayan didn't hear what Vatsala said. "What's the matter? Why aren't you talking?"

Not saying a word, Jayan kept walking with his head bowed.

"Why are you so serious today?"

Vatsala was surprised. Normally Jayan would talk constantly, burst out laughing, and wriggle out of her grasp to run through the street. He liked to throw rocks in the gutters.

Today, nothing like that happened.

By the time they reached school, the first bell had already rung.

Vatsala went with Jayan all the way up to his classroom door.

"Okay, I'm gonna go."

He nodded his head.

First period was Mr. Unni. He was Jayan's teacher.

"K. P. Mohanan!"

"Yes, sir." Mohanan stood up.

"M. Ramachandran!"

"Present, sir." Ramachandran stood up.

"M. P. C. Hasheem!"

"Yes, sir." Hasheem stood up.

"C. Jayan!"

When there was no reply, the teacher lifted his head from the register and looked out.

"C. Jayan!" Mr. Unni repeated.

There was no response.

"Are you sleeping over there?!"

The teacher stood up and went over to Jayan. Jayan was sitting down, his head just hanging.

"Aren't you feeling well?"

Jayan tossed his head indicating that nothing was wrong.

The teacher went back and sat down in his chair.

"Homework."

A murmur infected the children.

"Ashokan!"

Ashokan, who sat in the front row, dropped his head down. He hadn't done his homework.

Ashokan climbed up on top of the bench.

"Ramachandran!"

Ramachandran took his paper up to the teacher. The homework was just three problems. Two out of three were incorrect.

"Hasheem!"

Hasheem, too, took his paper up to the teacher. He had only done two of the problems. Both were wrong.

"Jayan!"

Jayan didn't hear what the teacher said.

"Jayan," the teacher repeated. Jayan didn't hear him. The teacher was puzzled for a moment. Finally, he stood up and walked over to Jayan.

"Didn't you do your homework?"

Jayan lifted his head and looked at the teacher. His eyes were raw and red.

The teacher took his paper and read it. He had done all three problems. All were correct.

"Smart boy—"

Jayan again dropped his head down. The teacher watched as tears filled his turbid eyes. Not understanding, the teacher looked long and hard at his face.

Mr. Unni rang the bell on top of his desk. The peon, Kanaran, came running.

"Kanaran, take Jayan back to his house."

"What's happened to him, sir?"

"A fever, I guess?"

Kanaran picked up Jayan's book and slate, took him by the hand, and went outside.

"Tell Sekharan that I'll be coming by this evening."

"I'll tell him, sir—"

Kanaran and Jayan exited to the street and started walking.

When they reached the main road, Jayan said softly, "I'll go by myself from here."

"I have to come, too. This street is filled with cars and buses." Kanaran lit a beedi cigarette.

"Please let go of me," Jayan begged Kanaran, staring at his face. His eyes overflowed with tears. Kanaran relaxed his grip.

Jayan walked to the edge of the road. Kanaran stood there nervously with the chewed beedi in his mouth, still holding Jayan's book and slate.

Jayan passed by the road to his house, crossed over a paddy field, and kept walking. The noon sun burned hot above him. His face sweltered in the heat.

Railroad tracks spread out before him. He sat down on the load-rest. His head drooped on his chest. The water from his eyes flowed down his cheeks.

Off in the distance, the *Mangalore Mail* was approaching. He drew closer to the railroad tracks. He laid himself face down on the ground. His tears fell on to the tracks and sizzled in the noon heat.

Spreading out smoke in all directions, shaking the earth, roaring hungrily, the train cut across the top of his head . . . .

They Are Singing

It was eight o'clock when he woke up.

Though he had opened his eyes, the kaleidoscopic sea did not vanish from his sight. In the weakness of his mind collapsed in a shallow sleep, multicolored waves caressed a sandy white beach.

He lay there smoking a cigarette with his eyes closed. O psychedelic dream, don't fade away. O colors, don't fade away.

Before waking up, he had seen a psychedelic dream. An ocean of many colors. A sea like the Pacific and Atlantic oceans come together—the Red Sea, the Black Sea, the Arabian Sea come together.

It was nine o'clock when he woke up.

It was eight o'clock when he woke up.

Though he had opened his eyes widely, the kaleidoscopic sea did not vanish from his sight. In the weakness of his mind collapsed in a shallow sleep, there were multicolored waves. Waves caressing a sandy white beach.

It was nine o'clock when he woke up.

He shaved his beard in a hurry. No time to brush his teeth or shower. He turned on the tap in the wash basin and quickly dunked his head. Crow's bath. Chinese bath. No time to eat breakfast. He poured the leftover tea down his throat. He threw on the shirt and pants he'd had dry cleaned yesterday. He took out a cigarette, lit it, and put it in his mouth. He locked his room and walked to the bus stand. No, he didn't walk. He galloped.

"Ten minute late, Babuji," the taxi-wallah said. He was an acquaintance. A dwarfish, white and red, middle-aged man. He's not supposed to be a taxi driver. He's a maharaja mistakenly born as a taxi driver.

No, he didn't walk. He galloped. He took out a cigarette, lit it; he locked his room and walked to the bus stand. He threw on the shirt and pants he'd had dry cleaned yesterday, and he poured the leftover tea down his throat. No time to eat breakfast. Chinese bath. Crow's bath. He turned on the tap in the wash basin and quickly dunked his head. No time to brush his teeth or shower. He shaved his beard in a hurry.

It was nine o'clock when he woke up.

"Namaste, sahib," said the peon who was standing watch in front of his office dressed in a Willie's shirt.

"Good morning, sir," said the young receptionist.

"Buenos días, Señor." Che Guevara's countryman, with red hair and eyes the color of honey, shook his hand.

"Como está Usted?"

It always made him shiver to hear that. The language Che Guevara spoke. Che Guevara's language.

He approached the desk and sat down. His desk. Red and green folders. A plastic holder he had made and painted himself out of a moped piston, filled with Charatat pens and pencils. He loved his desk. He loved everything and everyone. O Sun, I love you. O Septic Sewers, I love you. O Love, I love you.

Curls of long paper with red underlining and stars were coming out of the fax machine. It was for translating. Still he was in no mood to do the work. He looked at Domerg's *Nude*, which decorated the wall. He stood up and walked to the window. He looked outside. A peaceful, cloudless sky. A stiff breeze. He wanted to go out and follow the tracks of the ocean called the sky. Thinking his motivation to work would return if he smoked his pipe, he opened his can of tobacco, lit his pipe, and smoked.

He was not in the mood.

He picked up the telephone.

"Is that you?"

"Yeah."

Her warm voice from Ramakrishnapuram.

"What are you doing?"

"I'm reading."

He was not in the mood.

He picked up the telephone.

"Is that you?"

"Yeah."

Her warm voice from Ramakrishnapuram.

"I'm calling from the office. I don't feel like working."

"Why don't you feel like it?"

"Because I don't feel like it."

"Why is it that you don't feel like it because you don't feel like it?"

"It's because I don't feel like it that I don't feel like it because I don't feel like it."

A minute later, he asked, "Lemme come over, huh?"

"Now?"

Her surprise from the other end.

"Yeah, right now."

"Don't you have work to do?"

"May I never go to the office again."

May I never go to the office again. May I never go to the office again. May I never go to the office again.

He shaved his beard in a hurry. No time to brush his teeth or shower. He turned on the tap in the wash basin and quickly dunked his head.

"Ten minute late, Babuji."

He shaved his beard in a hurry.

"Which sari should I wear?"

"The one you bought a couple days ago."

"The one from Chanderi?"

"Yeah."

"Okay, see ya."

"See ya. Kisses."

"Kisses."

He put down the receiver. He grabbed his pipe and can of tobacco and went outside. He walked on the hot earth toward the taxi stand. This time it wasn't the maharaja mistakenly born as a taxi driver. An old guy the color of ganja with a beard.

"Which sari should I wear?"

"The one you bought a couple days ago."

"The one from Chanderi?"

At the edge of the street wrapped in a brown Chanderi sari she was waiting. Wrapped in a Chanderi sari she was waiting. Waiting.

"Why'd you quit work and rush over here?"

"Just to see you."

He wove his hand in between her slender fingers, in her slender fingers, in her slender fingers.

Walking.

"I saw a psychedelic dream today."

"Really?"

He told her about the psychedelic dream he had just before he woke up. She listened intently with amazement in her eyes.

Let me paint you a picture of the dream.

She can draw a picture today and call it "Psychedelic Ocean." Psychedelic Ocean. Ocean Psychedelic, Cean-o Chedelic-psy.

They walked along the side of the road and its racing rows of vehicles in single file. They must have gone to some little corner of the world where the roar of the cars and the stench of the gas couldn't reach. In the shadow of the Red Fort. In the desolation of the Kutub Minar. In the expanse of the India Gate.

He walked with his arm wrapped around her waist. He stopped under the lamppost and kissed her. The passersby stared.

"Again."

That's what she said when he touched her face. She lifted her face to him. Lips paled without lipstick. She lifted her face to him. That's what she said when he touched her face: "Again."

The passersby stared. He stopped under the lamppost and kissed her. He walked with his arm wrapped around her waist.

In the expanse of the India Gate. In the desolation of the Kutub Minar. In the shadow of the Red Fort.

In the shadow of the expanse. In the expanse of the desolation. In the expanse of the expanse and in the desolation of the desolation and in the shadow of the shadow. In the Red Fort of the Red Fort, in the Kutub Minar of the Kutub Minar. In the India Gate of the India Gate. In the Red Fort of the India Gate in the Kutub Minar of the Red Fort.

Because it was noon, Lodi Gardens was totally empty. They walked toward the sepulchers, trampling the shadows at the base of the scattered trees. Feeling her footsteps, the shadows soaked them up greedily. The shadows stuck to the bottom of her sandals like bits of dirt. And the bits of dirt on the bottom of her sandals spread out like shadows at the base of the trees.

Trampling the shadows . . . . . . .Sitting down on the crumbling steps of the sepulchers, he said:

"Sit next to me."

She obeyed. Her Chanderi sari spread out over the dilapidated steps. She took the end of her sari from her shoulder and let it fall over her head as she sat. Then she asked:

"Didn't Ibrahim Lodi die at Waterloo?"

"No, stupid, at Kurukshetra."

"Then who was it who retreated from Waterloo?"

"Herr Hitler."

"Who's Hitler?"

"You haven't heard of him?"

"No."

"He's the president of Cuba."

"Cuba's in South Africa, right?"

"South Africa?!" She was laughing, hidden in the long end of her unfurled sari.

"No, you idiot! Cuba's in the Middle East, near Egypt."

"Is de Gaulle the president now?"

"Of where?"

"Of Egypt?"

Though he never took his pipe from his mouth, a smile seeped onto his face.

"De Gaulle is the agricultural minister of Israel."

"Then who is the President of Egypt now?"

"Field Marshal Ayub Khan."

"Let's not talk for a while."

Agreed.

She shook her head in agreement.

Before waking up, he had seen a psychedelic dream. An ocean of many colors. A sea like the Pacific and Atlantic oceans come together—the Red Sea, the Black Sea, the Arabian Sea come together. Red, green, blue, and yellow waves, white, red, and blue sands.

"Let's not talk for a while."

"Agreed."

She shook her head in agreement.

Before waking up, he had seen a psychedelic dream.

"Let's not talk for a while."

"Agreed."

She shook her head in agreement.

Before waking up, he had seen a psychedelic dream.

He shaved his beard in a hurry. No time to brush his teeth or shower. He turned on the tap in the wash basin and quickly dunked his head.

He was not in the mood.

He picked up the telephone.

"Is that you?"

"Yes."

From Ramakrishnapuram turned on the tap in the wash basin to shower or brush his teeth of many colors in a hurry of Che Guevara who was mistakenly born as a taxi driver not walking in the weakness.

Let's not talk for a while.

"Not for just a while, forever."

She continued: "Let's die."

"Let's die."

Let's die. Let's die. Let's die.

He extinguished his pipe and put it in his pocket. He stood up from the steps. Along with her. Her Chanderi sari bloomed like a flower in the breeze.

They walked inside the sepulcher. The smell of time infested by termites. Faded red stones. They saw two cold, solid graves. A king's and a queen's. He climbed into the king's grave and lay down stretched out. As he lay down, he said:

"I died."

She climbed into the queen's grave and lied down. As she lay down, she said:

"I died, too."

They sang:

"We died."

Piss

Everyone was talking about the death of Kumaran Nayar. Kunyaman the tea stall guy says it was a murder. Vasu Kurup has the same opinion. In fact the majority of the locals believe it was murder.

"It was the Naxalites who killed him," Vasu Kurup said, his dark eyes staring straight at the sun.

"It wasn't no Naxalites that got him. It was a spirit. A ghost . . . " Kannan the Kolkali dancer disagreed.

Kumaran Nayar died in the cremation grounds. And it happened at dusk. He must have been caught up in the "arrival" of some spirit.

And so it was that people were saying all sorts of things about Kumaran Nayar's untimely death. I, too, had something to add. I said:

"It wasn't Naxalites that killed Kumaran Nayar. And it wasn't a spirit."

"Then who?"

They asked in unison. A look of nervous excitement came over their faces.

"I know who killed Kumaran Nayar. I alone . . . ."

Now they were really shocked. I repeated, "I alone . . . ."

"How do you know?" asked Vasu Kurup as he fixed his eyes on me, his sunlit violet eyes.

I didn't give a reply.

"Bullshit," said Kunyaman, "You don't know a thing."

Kunyaman mocked me. Only Kannan remained silent, sitting there with his legs crossed. He was staring at my face, his mouth halfway opened.

"Didja see it?"

Vasu Kurup's voice softened. His manner changed. He wanted to know the secret.

I'm a person without any secrets. My life is an open book. I don't want to conceal anything. And so I will tell you what I know about Kumaran Nayar's death. Kunyaman the tea guy, Vasu Kurup, and Kannan the Kolkali dancer might enjoy hearing it. The police at the Fifth Gate station might enjoy hearing it . . . .

Is there anybody who has never in their life borrowed some money? There comes a time when even rich people are forced into taking on a debt. At least once in their life. Through great perseverance I had managed to save up ten or twenty thousand rupees. It was all tucked away and protected in fixed deposits and the like. After I'm gone, my wife, Tangamani, my children Vatsan, Snehaprabha, Anilan, Pushpan—it was for them . . . .

Well, even though I had ten or twenty thousand rupees in savings, last Saturday I found myself in need of a hundred rupees.

I wrote out a check and sent Chattukutti off to the bank. I waited for him to return with the money.

"I didn't get the money. The bank's closed," Chattukutti said as he returned.

Then I remembered that today was a bank holiday. Tomorrow, Sunday, would be, too.

Chattukutti gave back the uncashed check.

After Chattukutti left, I sat down in the easy chair on the verandah and thought about the hundred rupees. I didn't notice that Tangamani had come out and was standing there next to me.

"What are you thinking about so intensely?"

She had just bathed and stood nearby covered in a black-bordered wrap with a black mark of sandal paste on her forehead. To see her you wouldn't think she'd had four children. If the circumstances had been different, I would have, I mean I might have, well . . . but right now my only thought was on that hundred rupees.

"I need a little money. How could I get it?"

She looked at me nervously. Why did I need money right now? And how much? Such were the questions contained in her glance.

"I need a hundred rupees."

"This is the big deal?" she laughed, "Did we somehow become desperate for money?"

"I need it by tomorrow morning, but the bank's closed today and tomorrow."

"What's so urgent?"

"I forgot to tell you. You know Rajasekharan from the office. Well, his wife gave birth. It was a C-section and, you know, he's got no money . . . ."

Rajasekharan had never borrowed money from me before. It's only because he's got no other way. Otherwise, I know he would never have asked me.

I gave my word that I'd bring it to him when I came by the office in the morning. Would he believe it if I said I didn't have it? And not just him, who would believe it, if you told them that a guy who'd held a good job for ten or twenty years didn't have a hundred rupees to lend?

"Do you have any cash on you, Tangamani?"

"Maybe twenty or twenty-five rupees. Do you want it?"

I've heard about a trick to make bills multiply. If only I knew the trick . . . .

Once again I sank deep into thought. And I think Tangamani started thinking about the hundred rupees business, too. She said:

"What about asking Master over there?"

I didn't respond.

"If we asked, he'd give it . . . ."

"Don't you think I know that, Tangamani? But who's gonna ask?"

Who's gonna tie the bell on the tomcat? How can I ask Master for the money? He's a respected man. Still . . . I have lived in this house for three years and four months. We see each other every day. We exchange pleasantries and nod our heads when we meet. But beyond that I don't know him at all.

That's just my nature. I shy away from getting close with other people. When I see people I know, I duck away and disappear. That's the secret of how I manage to live without friends in the city.

Except for my wife and my children, I don't have anyone to speak to openly. Kunyaman the tea guy, Vasu Kurup, and Kannan the Kolkali dancer aren't my friends, just acquaintances.

"Then ask Kumaran Nayar."

Tangamani saw a solution to the problem. She's certainly got street smarts.

So in the end that's how I decided to approach Kumaran Nayar for the money.

How many people are there in this area who haven't borrowed money from Kumaran Nayar? Rich people borrow thousands and tens of thousands from him. Middle class people, a hundred or two hundred. Of course, everyone gets an interest rate. And it's only after you've paid back the interest that you return the principal.

You must pay the money back on the stated date. Month after month the interest must be paid. Kumaran Nayar's a real stickler in such matters.

Kuttichattan was hired to bring Assu Mappila to his knees. When they drew the bucket from the well, human feces. When they went to make the rice, human feces. When they sat down to eat dinner, human feces. In the end, Assu Mappila went to Kumaran Nayar and clutched his feet. He paid back the money and the interest.

This was a long time ago, a story that happened before Tangamani and I came to this area. "Are you hesitant to ask Kumaran Nayar?"

Tangamani made me feel guilty. Actually I wasn't hesitant. He's a man who lends money. It's not like asking the Master in the neighborhood. Plus, it was only a matter of a hundred rupees. I would pay it back with interest the day after tomorrow.

When I went inside to get my shirt, I saw Kelappan coming with his spade on his shoulder. Fresh earth stuck to the sharp blade of his spade.

"Who died, Kelappa?"

"Madhavan the Yokel."

Madhavan was from someplace in another region. That's how he got the nickname "Yokel." He had no relatives or close friends. He lived in a crumbling backroom of an old shop in the market. He made a living carrying loads or working as a coolie.

"What'd he die from, Kelappa?"

"He been laid up coupla days now. It was cancer got him, what I heard."

My mind lit up with the image of Madhavan's thin black face strewn with grayed stubble.

"I've gotta go."

Kelappan put his spade on his shoulder and started walking. Bits of dirt fell from the sharp edge of his spade . . . .

Whenever someone died, it was Kelappan's job to prepare a hole at the cremation ground.

I grabbed my shirt and headed out.

When I approached Kumaran Nayar's house, my legs deadened. I had never in my life borrowed even a paisa until today. I am forty-five years old. But now . . . .

At that moment, I pictured Rajasekharan's wife sitting helplessly in the maternity ward. And with that my legs moved forward again.

If you exit the alley on the left side of the block office,

you're at Kumaran Nayar's house. Even though he lent money even to millionaires, you wouldn't think it if you saw his house. A middle-class hut. Everything thatched except for the verandah. The strong sunlight fell on top of the holes in the verandah.

When I entered, I saw that Kumaran Nayar was leaving. If I had delayed another couple of minutes, I would have missed him. It was lucky that I arrived when I did.

Pretending that he hadn't seen me, Kumaran Nayar exited the courtyard in a hurry. I was confused but remembered the fact that people who lend money on interest are crotchety. They are people who've lost their humanity. For whatever reason, they never hesitate, even to kill . . . .

"Sir, please wait a minute."

Kumaran Nayar just looked at me and then shot down the alley as though he hadn't heard what I said. There's another rotten thing about begging for money—the guy has to give a rat's ass.

It must have been an unconscious impulse that made me follow him quickly through the alley. Kumaran Nayar walked very deliberately without looking back. He was older than I, but he was also more active and healthy. And so in the blink of an eye, he was already in front of the block office.

I couldn't tolerate this disrespect. No one has ever treated me this way until today. But now this snooty, rich guy . . . I controlled myself. If I hadn't, I would have been sunk. Rajasekharan's wife's pale, pitiful face . . . .

I quickly entered the main road. I tied up my dhoti. Purposefully swinging his strong arms, Kumaran Nayar kept walking. He was muttering something to himself. Gnashing his teeth. Where was he going? What was he about to do? Why was he so rude to me? I didn't understand.

I followed him in fits and starts a few yards behind. The money I was to give to Rajasekharan was no longer the only thing on my mind. Without realizing it, a desire had grown in me, a desire to know what Kumaran Nayar was up to. I felt a second wind in my legs. A great leap or two and I was right behind him.

We bounded forward along the main road like two runners racing for the prize.

Suddenly Kumaran Nayar turned down another alley to the left. At the same speed, so did I. Now I could hear the sound of his breathing and see the sweat soaking the back of his neck.

A few seconds later I realized that he was walking through the alley that led to the cremation ground.

I guessed right. The small lane we were on ended in the middle of a cashew nut grove. With their heads hanging, the pendant bats in the cashew trees flapped their wings and flew off.

Kumaran Nayar entered the cremation ground. And I behind. The sun was about to set. A redness like a burning funeral pyre spread out through the cashew branches. I recognized the cremation mound of Yokel Madhavan, which hadn't lost the smell of fresh earth. And all around the footprints that still hadn't faded away.

Kumaran Nayar approached Madhavan's cremation mound. He was breathing heavily. Sweat dripped from his forehead and neck. Then he said something as he wrung his hands. I could clearly hear his biting bark:

"You couldn't have gone after you paid me, could you, you piece of shit?" Kumaran Nayar yelled, "You owed me three hundred rupees. You'll never make it to the next world, you bastard."

He hawked and spit toward Madhavan's chest. But not content, he lifted the front part of his dhoti. With a shiver, the yellow liquid fell onto the new earth . . . .

My body trembled from head to toe. My eyes and ears burned. A large, sharp piece of granite appeared in my hand. All I remember is leaping forward with the stone.

When I came to my senses, I saw Kumaran Nayar lying face down in his own blood and piss.

Breast Milk

This being her third pregnancy, she was exhausted. Her face was a pale yellow. Even a simple walk winded her. She couldn't do any work. She was constantly lying down. Then she couldn't even get down from the bed. So she went to see a lady doctor. Her husband went along with her. The doctor checked her with a stethoscope and took her to lie down behind a blue screen. The doctor examined her thoroughly and then asked:

"Is your oldest child still taking breast milk?"

"Yes."

"How old is he?"

"He'll be four on the tenth of Vrischyam."

"Don't feed the older one breast milk anymore."

She shook her head in acknowledgment.

"Just shaking your head isn't good enough. Did you understand what I said? Only give breast milk to your youngest."

The doctor took a stethoscope and checked her once more, then wrote out a prescription for some pills called Septilin.

"Take two of these pills three times a day," the doctor said.

"Before or after eating?" she asked.

"After eating is fine."

"With fresh water or boiled water?" she asked.

"Go ahead and take it with cooled boiled water."

She took the prescription for the medication. Her husband took some money from the fold in his dhoti and gave it to the doctor. The doctor took the money and put it on the table. She and her husband left. They walked toward town. They bought the pills from the pharmacy. Fifty pills in a yellow bottle. Her husband tied up his dhoti and walked on. Short of breath, she followed behind. She said to no one in particular: "If he were a child who ate congee and rice, it would have been no problem, but besides breast milk is there anything that will stay in his stomach?"

She was talking about her oldest child, about Raju. He was four. He didn't like congee and rice. He liked breast milk. If he didn't get it even once, there would be hell to pay. Raju was sleeping when she went to the doctor that morning. She knew he wouldn't drink any congee or tea. That he would be waiting for her breast milk. She increased the speed of her gait. She said to herself: "My Raju must be starving. It's already ten! His insides must be all dried out, Guruvayurappa!"

"He's four, isn't he? How can he keep drinking breast milk?" her husband said. He took a beedi out of the fold in his dhoti and lit it. She didn't say anything. Because she was exhausted, her mind just kept brooding on Raju.

"It'll just take a couple of days of eating congee and rice to get him used to it. If you want, I'll get him some bitter aloes from the Mussad's store," her husband continued as he released the smoke through his nose.

"He doesn't need any of that. He doesn't need any aloes. Don't you think he'll understand what's going on if we talk about that?"

She thought about Raju the whole way home, talked about him. The alley ended. They came to the path through the paddy field. She could see the gate of their house in the distance. She saw the front of the house. When she came near, she saw Raju sitting in the threshold. All of a sudden she spoke. "Let Raju have the breast milk, too. Bring on whatever illness may come as a result. Whatever Guruvayurappan has fated will happen, no one can stop it."

"What are you talking about, Janu? Are you crazy? What'd

the doctor tell you? You aren't even able to get up and walk around. You've got to remember that we have two kids here whose arms and legs aren't tired out," her husband admonished. He took out another beedi and lit it.

She and her husband came through the gate and entered the courtyard. Raju was sitting in the threshold. His face looked withered. He was wearing black knickers with a vine design but no shirt. His little belly had shriveled up.

"Didn't my little boy have some congee?" she asked as she quickly ascended the stone steps leading to the threshold.

He didn't speak. He sucked his fingers as he sat on the floor spread with cow dung. She kissed his cheek.

"It's eleven. My little boy hasn't eaten his congee. O dear Guruvayurappa."

Hearing the noise, her mother came out from the kitchen.

"Your rascal is awfully stubborn. He doesn't want congee, he doesn't want roti. Such pigheadedness! He's like a Gandhari!"

"Why didn't you eat your congee, boy?" his father asked.

He didn't speak. He just kept sucking his fingers with a smack.

"Come here, little one. Why don't you have your congee?"

She grabbed him and picked him up.

He said, "No congee, milk."

"Milk?! There won't be any more milk. Already four years old, and he wants milk! Get over there and drink your congee," his father said. He yanked him by the hand and dragged him to the kitchen. His congee was still there in the bowl. His father sat him down in front of it. He didn't touch the congee. Tears welled up as he said:

"Milk! I want milk."

"Your mother can't give you milk anymore. The doctor said, 'Don't give your boy milk anymore.'"

She drew the congee from the bowl with a spoon and put it to his mouth. He turned his face away. Acting like he hadn't heard what she said, he stared at her breast and said:

"Milk."

"Milk! I'm gonna give you a swift kick! Drink your congee. I said drink it!"

His father pinched his ear. He let out a scream and started to cry.

"Have you lost it? Are you crazy?" her mother said.

Raju just cried louder. She said:

"Okay, okay. You can drink Mother's milk for just one more day, but starting tomorrow, no more milk, got it?"

She picked him up and put him in her lap. She started unbuttoning her blouse. Raju suddenly stopped crying.

"Janu!" her husband cried. His voice was angry. His face red. He stared at her fiercely. She was overwhelmed. He continued:

"If you get sick again, then you just go rest your little head and leave the rest of us to deal with it. You certainly are great at making everyone else miserable. I know you."

He grabbed the keys. Angrily he descended the steps and went off toward the shop. She didn't give Raju her milk. She didn't know what to do. She started crying and when Raju saw her crying, he started crying again. Her mother said:

"What is this? Has your mother died, that you're sitting here crying like this?"

She wiped her tears away. She took Raju and went to the front of the house. She tried to make him understand. He was a smart boy. If she told him, he would understand. When his obstinate phase was over, he would drink congee, she decided.

When school let out at noontime, her younger brother came by—Gopi. He washed his hands and face and pulled a stool into the kitchen—Gopi. Next to him, she brought in a stool for Raju. She put his congee bowl in front. Then she went and got Raju. She sat him on the stool. His belly was shrinking up. His eyes sank. She served some rice in his bowl.

She said, "Let's see who can eat first? Who's gonna win, Uncle Gopi or you? C'mon."

He didn't say a word. She continued:

"Oh, Uncle Gopi's flying. He's gonna win. Hurry up, eat it, if you wanna beat Uncle Gopi. Hurry."

She squeezed the rice into a ball and put it to his mouth. He turned his head away.

"Do you know how happy Mommy would be if you'd just eat this little bit, sweetie? Try a little, just a bite."

She begged him. He didn't play along. Without saying anything, she pounded the doorjamb. Raju sat on his stool and cried. What if she just put him in her lap and gave him some milk? She'd thought of it many times, but then she'd remember her husband's red face. She'd hear his angry voice. She didn't dare. She picked Raju up. She went to the front of the house. She stroked his hair with her fingers as she sat. Then her younger baby woke up crying. She sat Raju on the bench and went to her little child.

Raju sat on the bench, his face sweating. Kalyani was lying down in the corner of verandah—the dog. She'd just given birth. Four pups. The babies were sucking the teats swollen with milk.

She seated her infant in her lap and loosed the buttons on her blouse. The baby grasped her chest with its hand. It suckled her breast with its eyes half-closed. She felt Raju's torment-filled eyes creeping over from the porch. The baby took the milk from just one breast. That was enough. Its stomach full, the baby fell back asleep.

"Janu, aren't you gonna eat or drink anything today?"

"I'm not hungry."

"How could you not be hungry? What have you eaten?"

"Well, if Raju doesn't eat anything?"

"When you're hungry, you should eat. If I'm hungry, my arms and legs get tired."

She didn't eat. Raju went to sleep. She laid him down in the bed. She lay down beside him. She touched her face to his, stained with the dried salt of his tears. Why did she go see the doctor? She shouldn't have gone. My son is starving because I went, she thought. She loathed her husband. It was he who took her to the doctor after all.

"Did the boy eat something?"

"Mother and child are fasting," her mother said.

He gnashed his teeth.

"He didn't eat, did he? Where is he? I'll show him."

He dashed inside. Raju was sleeping. His father jerked him up and raised his rough hand. Raju, who hadn't fully woken up, cried out. Again and again he lifted his hand.

"Have you killed my son?! Have you killed him?!" she cried out desperately.

"Shut up. You better shut up. Janu, I told you to shut up."

She cried out again. Hearing the commotion, the little one woke up. Now he, too, was crying.

"Serve the meal," he said to her mother.

He hung Raju under his arm and carried him toward the kitchen.

"What is this madness? You're gonna kill that child."

"Didn't I tell you to serve dinner?"

He clenched his teeth. He threw Raju on the stool. She served the rice. He shoved the bowl in front of him and said:

"Eat."

He didn't move.

"I said eat."

"Milk . . . ."

The blood raced to his face. His eyes narrowed. His lips quivered. Insane rage seized him. Again he hung Raju under his arm and plunged into the next room. She covered her eyes and ears.

"O my Guruvayurappa . . . ."

Her mother cried out, too.

When his hand cramped up, he came out. He went straight to the front porch and lay down on the bench. The rice had cooled in the pot. No one ate. The lamp was doused. The house sank in darkness. In one bed, she and the little one. In the other, her husband and Raju. She couldn't hear Raju breathing. Was he asleep? Neither did she hear her husband. The embers from the beedi he had been smoking shone in the darkness. Only her sighing broke the silence of the room. The beedi's embers died out. He rolled over and started snoring.

Slowly Raju sat up in the bed. The room was pitch black. He

climbed over his father and got down. Groping in the darkness, he found his mother's bed. He felt for the top and climbed in. He fumbled over his mother's body with his hands. His hands stopped at her chest. He lifted her blouse and greedily pressed his mouth against her breast—

"Where's the boy?"

He jumped up. A scratch of the matchbox. A red light glimmered. He clenched his teeth.

"Didja get enough, you?"

He pulled Raju down. Raju cried. She cried. The baby woke up and cried out. Again a great uproar. In the middle of the night, he took the mattress and blanket from his own bed and spread them out on the verandah. He dragged Raju outside and laid him down. Then he said:

"Close the door and bolt it."

Her mother closed the door and bolted it from the inside.

With an air of victory, he lay down on his mattress. Near Raju the starlight shone on the porch. A cold wind blew. He covered himself with the blanket.

Sunrise. A blue light filled the porch. He moved his father's coarse arm and slowly got out from under the blanket. Without a sound he walked along the front of the house. In a corner of the verandah the dog and her puppies were sleeping. On a spread-out sack they slept. In the blue light he could see the dog's teats plump with milk. He bent over next to the dog . . . .

I, the Scavenger

I just got a job as a scavenger under the auspices of the Delhi Municipal Corporation.

A big-shot official named Mr. Shishupalan in an office got the job for me.

Even now I remember the day I got the job. It's very clear. I haven't forgotten a thing. On that day, my legs were trembling, my mind racing.

I stood propped up against a post in the courtyard outside Mr. Agarwal's office. I was nervous and apprehensive. I was about to start a job for the first time in my life. And a government job at that. I watched the other scavengers come and go from my perch on the pillar. All the scavengers were pictures of exhaustion. The eyes of the older ones had yellowed. The color of filth. Theirs was a distant look. (I found out later that they looked that way because they smoked hash.) I stood outside the office, nerves rattling for an hour or two.

Just as it was about noon, Mr. Agarwal stuck his head out and yelled, "All right, asshole, get in here."

When I heard that, I was a little relieved. Still, I couldn't shake my nervousness. What was Mr. Agarwal going to do? What all would he instruct me to do? Trying to control myself, I stepped out onto the verandah. Squatting there were a few scavengers smoking beedis. I noticed them staring at me with interest. They were all wearing khaki shirts and short pants.

That, of course, is the scavenger's uniform. When I recall that I am able to wear that same uniform, I feel tremendous joy.

Mr. Agarwal sat on top of a packing crate. He didn't have a uniform. His dress was a white-collared, stitched-together shirt splattered with mud and shit. A mass of hairs had jungled on his face.

I walked up to Mr. Agarwal and bent over to touch his feet.

He gave me the once over. Scratching his beard, he asked, "What's your name, asshole?"

I said my name. Once again, I touched his feet worshipfully.

In front of Mr. Agarwal stood an old desk with only three legs. He took a yellow piece of paper from the top of the desk, shoved it toward me, and demanded:

"Sign it."

I took the paper and looked at it—it had a bunch of Hindi and Urdu written all over it. I tried to read it, separating out each letter and word. Mr. Agarwal jumped up with a bark.

"What the fuck are you doing, asshole? Look, we got us a bookworm!"

"Forgive me—"

I was frightened by Mr. Agarwal's anger. He was my provider. It was thanks to his kindness that I would regularly be drinking congee from now on.

"Forgive me—"

I pleaded once again. Mr. Agarwal snatched the paper from my hands, slammed on the table, and said, "Sign here."

I put my signature at the spot he pointed out.

"Hey, Fulram!"

Fulram, who was crouched near the wall, leaped up.

"Go with Fulram here. He'll explain everything."

Bent over on my knees at Mr. Agarwal's feet, I touched the crown of my head to his sandals with the broken strap.

"Get out of here—" Mr. Agarwal ordered.

I got up and walked out with Fulram. He walked toward a narrow, poorly lit room. There were five or six pairs of uniforms, a bunch of brooms, and some waste bins.

"Find a shirt that fits and put it on . . . " Fulram said. I looked over the uniforms one by one. They were all used and ragged. All of them were ripped and soiled with dirt and shit. I selected a shirt and shorts. As Fulram instructed, I changed into my uniform right there.

Grabbing a waste bin from among those set in the room, Fulram said: "Here, take this one, asshole."

I took the waste bin.

"A broom?" I gently inquired. Fulram grabbed a broom, too, and gave it to me.

Bin and broom in hand, uniform on, we left Mr. Agarwal's office and I sighed with relief and delight.

"Arjuna!" Fulram yelled. Sitting on the porch, smoking a beedi, Arjunan got up and came over.

"You go with him . . . " Fulram commanded me as he pointed to Arjunan.

I walked with Arjunan, holding my bin and broom.

I had become a scavenger.

I had become a human being.

With elation, I took another deep breath.

Arjunan led me to a subdivision called Kashiram Village. It was a subdivision with cracked alleys and tired buildings. Old men on charpoys smoked hookahs in the busy alleyways. Children in lines were deserting the edges of the streets. Every inch was soaked in unbearable stench.

A municipal toilet stood in the open space at the intersection of two alleys.

"You're in charge of this," Arjunan said.

Businessmen were lined up around the toilet, fruits and vegetables discarded. Half-eaten chola batura and other assorted foodstuffs.

Arjunan approached the front of the toilet and crowed, "Anybody in there?"

A couple of girls cooed.

"Well, hurry up!" Arjunan demanded.

Within five minutes, two or three girls emerged with pots in their hands. Spreading the stench as they walked by, the girls stared straight at me. I was a new scavenger all right.

"Only girls shit here," said Arjunan, "Men and children just crap on the street."

Arjunan bummed a beedi off me and bid me farewell when he finished it.

I entered the toilet. There was a putrid stench. I cleaned the toilet by pouring water around, brushing it with my broom, and wiping it down.

Besides the one in Kashiram Village, I was in charge of just two other toilets. After tidying up those toilets as well, I lit a beedi and started to walk. Bin and broom in hand, body covered in filth, wafting a stink as I walked, I couldn't help but think of Mr. Shishupalan. Without his help, how could I ever have gotten this job? He was my savior. With Mr. Shishupalan's help and through the grace of Lord Rama, I have become a scavenger. I have become a human being.

On my return, I saw Arjunan waiting for me. On his instructions, I entrusted my bin and broom to Fulram. As we left, Arjunan asked, "Where do you live?"

I gave no reply. Even now I myself didn't know where I lived.

"Don't you have a home?"

"No."

I had never thought about a house before. But from now on, I must. I mean, I'm a government official now, after all.

"Don't you have anybody?"

"My mother is dead. My father's in jail."

"No brothers or sisters?"

"No."

Arjunan bummed another beedi off me. He sent the smoke soaring and said, "Why don't you stay with me, if you don't have any objection?"

I did not have one objection. I walked with him. Arjunan talked the whole way without taking a breath. About Mala Sinha and Helen. About transistor radios. And about Holi.

And so it was that from that day forward I started to live with Arjunan. He was alone. His family lived in some village near Panipat. Once a month he would hop a thieves' train to see his wife and children.

Arjunan had seen every Hindi film ever made. He would go to restaurants to eat. He would smoke cigarettes.

He was a big shot.

Everyday Arjunan would buy and drink some arrack in the late afternoon.

He was a drinker.

I didn't usually go to movies. Didn't smoke cigarettes regularly. Didn't drink much.

Arjunan lived in a shack constructed of tarpaulin and sacks. There was nothing in the shack, except for a charpoy and a clay pot for drinking water.

As the months went by and I received my pay, I bought a little stove and some pans. And so in the evenings after work was over, I would cook. I'd make some roti and vegetables quite early and then go to bed. Arjunan would see a movie, hang out with his friends, and come home in the middle of the night. Even though I always prepared enough roti and vegetables for him, he never ate any of it, not even once.

Two or three years passed like this.

One day Arjunan brought home a marriage proposal for me. She was the daughter of Ramu Lal, another scavenger who worked under Mr. Agarwal; her name was Fulbatti. Arjunan said, "It's a first-class proposal. You'd get three hundred rupees and a transistor radio as dowry. What do you say?"

"If you like it, I do."

Arjunan gave me a big hug and kissed me on the cheeks.

His lip was like a millipede.

"Let's arrange it before Dussera."

Arjunan spoke to Ramu Lal. The next day, Ramu Lal's man brought me a new shirt and short pants. Plus, a kilo of the sweets called burfi.

"You're a lucky guy."

Arjunan hugged me again.

Our marriage did indeed take place before Dussera. Dressed in new clothes, my head bedecked with garlands of flowers, riding on horseback—like everyone is at his marriage—I went to Fulbatti's hut. Drinking up the rhythm of the band, losing consciousness, Arjunan and his friends danced Bhangra.

Fulbatti was a ten- or fifteen-year-old, blossoming young child.

In my mind, never fading, never forgetting, that night holding her, sleeping with her, pressing my hands reeking with the stench of the toilet to her breast.

The next year, Fulbatti gave birth.

The year after that, she gave birth . . .

I love my wife, Fulbatti, and my children Mandu, Kakku, and Munni more than life.

As far as I'm concerned, all women are Fulbattis. All children are Mandus, and Kakkus, and Munnis.

As far as I'm concerned, the world's toilets are my home.

As the Vavs and Dusseras passed by, I noticed a change coming over the color of my face. One day I looked at my reflection in a mirror shard splattered with mud. My face was yellow. In my eyes, too, a yellow.

The color of filth.

As I got older, I started smoking hash like the rest of the scavengers. Eating pakoras laced with hash, resting my youngest child on my lap, I was sitting on the charpoy in front of the hut. It was then that I spotted Mr. Shishupalan walking by.

I was thrilled to see him. Many years had passed, a couple of decades it seemed, since I had seen him. Even though it had been such a long time, I had no trouble at all recognizing him.

I fell at Mr. Shishupalan's feet.

"Please stand up," he instructed.

"Come with me."

He commanded, before I was able to say anything. I was his dependent. I was so deeply indebted to him.

Mr. Shishupalan started walking. Head bowed behind him, I, his dependent, walked. I didn't pay attention to where we were going. But I knew that he was walking through the alleys toward the cremation ground.

River and Boat

"Are you ready, Bhaskaran?" Uncle asked. "We have to leave before Rahu."

"It's already past eight," Father said.

"Bhaskaran!" Uncle yelled.

"Bhaskaran's upstairs," Radha said.

Father went upstairs and entered Bhaskaran's room. He was squatting in a chair, his head in his hands. His dull, uncombed hair was strewn across his forehead. His eyes were morning red. He didn't sleep at all the night before.

"Bhaskaran," Father said quietly, "Don't you want to take a bath?"

"Mm," he said without lifting his face from his hands.

"C'mon, go take a bath. We should head out before Rahu."

He got up from the chair. Father walked behind him. Together they went downstairs.

"Radha, bring a towel and some oil for Bhaskaran."

Radha took out a towel and a little oil.

"Well, go shower," Uncle said impatiently.

Bhaskaran walked toward the bathroom. He looked at the face in the mirror hanging on the wall—his face. The languor of sleep had solidified in his eyes. Blue hair had crept across his face.

He didn't shave yesterday.

He didn't eat. He didn't sleep.

"Bhaskar-etta," Radha asked, "do you want some hot water to shave with?"

"Mm."

Radha went into the kitchen to heat up some water.

"If you have to shave, Bhaskaran, make it quick. We should leave before Rahu," Uncle reminded him.

Radha brought the hot water. Bhaskaran took it and walked into the bathroom.

Every day this younger sister brought her brother water to shave. Will there be any need to do it anymore? Will there be any need tomorrow?

Tears welled up in Radha's eyes.

"I don't have an ounce of peace about this whole thing," Father said, "When I think about Bhaskaran's mother, I just can't . . . no peace, you know . . . it's a . . . "

"It's all according to fate, Kunnikrishnan," Uncle said in a tone of utter helplessness.

Bhaskaran's mother was lying down.

She had been lying down since yesterday.

She didn't bathe.

She didn't eat.

She didn't sleep.

Uncle went into her room. She lay there with loosened hair and tremulous eyes. The grand lady of the neighborhood lay on the floor near the legs of the bed, her grayed eyes filled with tenderness and sorrow.

She didn't see Uncle come in. Uncle softly called to her, "Lakshmi."

She sobbed when she heard his voice. Her shoulders heaved.

"What good will sitting here crying like this do—not eating anything, not drinking anything? It's all according to Guruvayurappan's will."

"My Bhaskaran . . . " Mother sobbed.

"What will Bhaskaran think if he sees you crying all curled up like this? Don't cause his heart any more pain, Lakshmi."

"Don't make everyone else suffer either, Lakshmi," Father added, "Get up and eat something. Put on a smile and say goodbye to your son."

Without saying a word, Mother continued to cry. Father put his hand on her shoulder and said, "Please get up, Lakshmi. It's me talking. Get up."

Gently drying her grayed eyes, he said, "Get up, dear. It's Bhaskaran's father speaking. Stand up, dear."

"My Bhaskaran . . . " Mother cried, "He's the only son I have. O great Goddess! If anything should happen to Bhaskaran . . . "

She couldn't stop. She convulsed and wept in fleeting gasps of breath.

"Lakshmi, he told you to get up," Uncle said in a serious voice.

Slowly she stood, only to sit down again. She started to cry again.

"Dear, will you bring Lakshmi something to drink?" Father asked the servant who was standing in the shadow of the door.

The servant wiped her eyes as she walked toward the kitchen.

Bhaskaran shaved.

He showered.

And then he came out. It appeared as though the light in his eyes had returned. Now it was curly, glistening hair strewn across his forehead.

Mother burst into tears when she saw him.

Bhaskaran approached his mother. He squeezed her shoulder. He tried to comfort her, saying, "Mom, why are you crying? Nothing's going to happen to me. I'm coming back tomorrow . . . "

"Radha, will you bring the stools in and serve the rice?"

Radha brought the stools and put them around the table.

"Sit down. C'mon, sit down. We have to remember to leave here before Rahu," Uncle told everyone. He sat down.

Bhaskaran sat.

Father sat.

Radha served the rice. First, Uncle's plate. Then, Father's plate. Finally, Bhaskaran's.

Her hand trembled as she scooped the rice onto Bhaskaran's plate.

Uncle poured some sambar into the mouth of his volcano of rice. He rolled and squeezed the rice into big fists and devoured them.

Father picked out the peanuts from his curry and swallowed them like pills.

Bhaskaran just looked at his plate.

"What's the matter, Bhaskaran?" Uncle asked.

"Yes, why aren't you eating?" Mother sobbed as she leaned in the doorway.

Uncle emptied his plate.

Father and Bhaskaran had also had enough.

Bhaskaran took some water from the spouted jug and washed his face. He saw Joseph and Usman coming.

Joseph and Usman were Bhaskaran's classmates.

They work together in the same office. Bhaskaran tried to smile when he saw his friends.

"Are you ready to go?" Joseph asked.

"Mm."

"Di-did you, uh . . . eat lunch?" Usman stutteringly inquired.

Bhaskaran put on his freshly laundered dhoti and shirt.

He combed his hair.

Put on his sandals.

"Well? Shall we go?" Uncle asked.

"Say goodbye, son!" Father said.

Bhaskaran approached his mother, "Okay, Mom, I've gotta go. I'll be back tomorrow."

Mother hugged Bhaskaran. She nestled her face into his chest and wept.

The Great Goddess pulled her away from him.

"See you soon, sis," Bhaskaran said goodbye to Radha. She bit her lips and held back her tears.

"Take that first step and go, kid," Uncle instructed Bhaskaran.

Having said his farewells, Bhaskaran stepped outside. The murmur of the crowd outside rose into a clamor.

"Nothing's going to happen to Bhaskar-ettan. Something tells me . . . no danger will befall him." Radha said to herself amidst her sobs.

Uncle walked in front. Behind him, Father. Usman and Joseph walked side by side with Bhaskaran.

The sunlight began to fade. The sky dimmed.

All the neighbors were standing on their front porches waiting to see Bhaskaran go.

"It's the boy's destiny. He's only twenty-four years old. And this . . . well . . . "

"He's Lakshmi-amma's only son."

Following his uncle, Bhaskaran walked with his father and his friends.

They passed through the streets and alleys.

In the distance, they could see the cremation ground and the black smoke rising up from the burning pyres.

They saw Kuttan Pillai waiting in front of the cremation ground underneath a cashew tree.

They stopped when they reached the cashew tree.

"Kuttan Pillai," Uncle said, "this is Bhaskaran. Here he is."

Kuttan Pillai turned around. He was a short, fat bear. The hairs on his swollen feet twisted and twined like slender worms. His eyes were burning coals. A bag hung from his shoulder.

People always called him Kalan Kuttan Pillai, the herald of death.

"Go, son. It's all according to fate," Uncle said.

"We're optimists, Bhaskaran. Nothing's gonna happen. You'll come back safely," his friends said.

"Kuttan Pillai, we're putting Bhaskaran in your hands. Bhaskaran is his mother's only son," Father said.

Kuttan Pillai said nothing.

When Bhaskaran finished saying goodbye to everyone, Kuttan Pillai gave the order: "Walk."

The snake birds resting in the cashew tree flew off in fear when they heard Kuttan Pillai's corpulent growl.

Bhaskaran bowed his head and followed Kuttan Pillai.

Kuttan Pillai walked along the long, deserted path. Bhaskaran followed.

The path ended in a wasteland. An unpopulated land, a thick carpet of decayed shrubbery, and withered palm trees. Vultures crouched on the peaks of the dried palms.

The palm trees gradually faded away. The thicket disappeared.

Kuttan Pillai walked through the endless expanse of wasteland. Bhaskaran followed.

A wasteland without beginning or end. Four corners, four horizons infinitely sloping away.

With his dhoti pulled up, fat legs covered with hair, and sick grin, Kuttan Pillai walked tirelessly on like a dumb ox.

Walking and walking, Bhaskaran tired. His legs ached. He gasped for breath. The straps of his sandals sawed into his flesh. Bhaskaran had to run to catch up with Kuttan Pillai.

Never looking back, never speaking, Kuttan Pillai set his sights on the horizon before him and just walked.

The sun set. A hazy darkness ensued. Far off in the distance, he heard the sound of a river rippling and toppling onto itself. Bhaskaran realized that his journey was about to end.

They were reaching their destination.

The ripple of the water became a roar.

Bhaskaran stared at the huge river that emanated from the shadowy horizon and flowed across to the opposite horizon.

Here it is, moments of time passing before him.

Darkness covered everything. He could not see Kuttan Pillai.

"Here, this is your boat," Kuttan Pillai's voice called from the darkness.

Groping around the blackness, Bhaskaran discovered his boat. A small boat. And a single oar.

"Get in."

Kuttan Pillai's voice rang out.

Bhaskaran got in the boat.

Kuttan Pillai reached in his bag and pulled out a clock. He looked at the time. Midnight. Twelve o'clock.

He had to reach the other shore before twelve-thirty. He had to come back before one.

Kuttan Pillai pushed the boat into the shouting river and disappeared into the darkness.

Drenched in black, the screaming river spread out before Bhaskaran. He could not see the other shore. Whirlpools sucked and spun at the speed of light. Tongues of rippling water licked the sky. Sea elephants hissed and screamed, tearing their mouths. Water snakes slithered and curled.

Bhaskaran took the oar in his hand. Would he reach the other shore? Would he return?

The Seventh Flower

It was their first night. He regaled her with stories until midnight. The variegated experiences of a life.

When he told her the story of how in his childhood he climbed a young calf and tried to ride it, she shook with laughter.

When he told her about all the struggles he had faced searching for work abroad, her eyes teared up.

And when he told about all the passion he felt for a young girl with long hair from the editorial department at his office, she bit her bottom lip so hard it bled.

Toward the end, when the midnight crow called out, he said:

"Now you tell me something, Sujata."

"About what?"

"About anything," he said as he lay down, nestling his head on her left arm, "Some experience in your life."

She had a gold necklace around her neck. Inside the locket was a little picture of Lord Unnikrishnan. Resting in the Pipal leaves, sucking his thumb, crowned with a peacock feather—Unnikrishnan.

"Let me tell you about this locket, then?"

"Okay, go ahead."

He took out a cigarette from right where he was lying and lit it.

"Can I go pick some flowers?"

Chitra and Vatsan were waiting for her in the street, on the other side of the painted green gate.

They were both younger than Sujata. Chitra was in the eighth grade. Her little brother, Vatsan, was in the sixth.

Hearing what Sujata had said, her mother raised her head from the weekly magazine she was reading and asked, "How old are you?"

A college girl going to pick flowers—

"I won't go anymore. But just for today . . . ." she pleaded. That's how much Sujata loved to pick flowers.

Every Onam, she would take a flower basket and go out to Vannanpara to pick flowers. For two years, this habit had been interrupted because she was growing up.

Chitra and Vatsan were waiting anxiously beyond the gate. Sujata feared they might go off without her.

As she came home from college that morning, she and Chitra ran into each other.

Chitra asked, "Checci, don't you wear flowers anymore?"

"I don't have a little brother to go picking flowers with." The pain of being without a brother sounded in her voice.

"Why don't you come along with us, Checci?"

She sighed when she heard that. Memories of lost youth somewhere behind . . .

"So, will you come with us tomorrow, Checci?"

"Where?"

"Vannanpara."

"Okay, I'll come." The response just came out without a thought.

"Go ahead," said her mother, "but make sure you're back before sundown. If your father finds out, I'll never hear the end of it."

Sujata didn't hear those last words. She was already at the gate before they were uttered.

Chitra and Vatsan were very happy. They gave Sujata a flower basket. The three quickly set out for Vannanpara.

The tumba flowers were stacked up around the edge of the paddy field. The paddy waters mixed with manured soil swelled the violet crow flowers. She swung her basket as he she walked, noticing the tinkling sound of the anklets on her feet . . . .

In the old days, too, she had worn anklets on her feet. She would listen to the jingling as she went here and there. But then she lost her anklets when she was ten.

"You're getting older," her mother said, "you shouldn't wear anklets anymore."

When her mother unclasped the anklets from her feet, she couldn't control her tears. She lost her youth that day along with her anklets.

She saw some other children there when they came near Vannanpara. Everyone had flower baskets in their arms. Like a butterfly she flew across the tops of the tumba flowers and the crow flowers.

Gradually, Vannanpara shimmered like gold in the fading sunlight. Darkness spread through the forest of creeping vines at the edge of the rocks.

Tomorrow she would decorate the courtyard with flowers of the seven colors. When her mother and father woke up, the first sight they'd see would be her flower arrangement. Her basket overflowed with tumba flowers and crow flowers.

"Checci, it's time to go."

Vatsan was frightened at seeing the darkening sky.

"The conch is blowing in the temple. C'mon."

Sujata didn't hear. She only had six kinds of flowers in her basket. She still needed one more.

"I'm scared." Vatsan was frightened when he heard the cry of the waterfowl from somewhere.

"C'mon, let's go."

"Wait, kids," said Sujata, "I'll be right there."

Searching for the seventh flower, Sujata crossed into the dense grove of creeping vines. Chitra and Vatsan got scared when they saw her. They had never gone inside the creeper forest. They were afraid even to walk near it.

Inside the creeper forest, there were vines like snakes every-where. The children didn't know where the creeper forest ended. A long time ago a brave child went inside, but he never came back out afterward . . . .

A soft, red light and behind it darkness fell over the creeper forest. Standing inside, Sujata was plucking and picking spit-toon flowers and putting them in her basket.

But she still didn't have the seventh flower.

"Checci, come on!" Chitra and Vatsan were yelling from outside, "We're getting scared!"

The rest of the children who had come to pick flowers had already left.

Sujata loosened the tangled creepers and moved in deeper. They were the kind of vines that lacked any leaves. The creep-ers floated and played all around her like strands of hair. She felt as though she was moving through a clump of swamp grass.

A little further on, right in the middle of all the creepers, suddenly a light shined. Her eyes yellowed. A castle in the mid-dle of the creepers. Its walls, pillars, and arches were gilded with gold. The creeping vines hung down from the golden walls.

"Welcome, young lady," said someone from inside the castle.

She got scared and froze.

"Please come in."

A rough, male voice.

She stood hesitant without moving forward.

All of a sudden a huge figure appeared in the golden door. He was extraordinarily large. She thought he must be a demon. Except for some vines that hung around his waist, he had no other clothes on his body.

"Please come in, young lady."

Trudging through the mess of creepers she approached him. She had never been afraid of demons. The demon escort-ed her inside the castle.

"What is your name?"

"Sujata. I'm in my first year of pre-degree."

He took a handful of flowers from the basket on her arms and smelled them.

"Don't you want to know who I am?"

"Are you a demon?"

She stared at his huge face with curiosity.

"Yes, I'm the demon of the creeper forest. This is my castle."

Next he proceeded to give her a tour of the entire castle. The ornamentation inside amazed her. The chairs, the beds, everything was cast in gold.

The demon rested on his enormous throne. He seated Sujata in a chair in front of him.

"You're the first girl ever to enter inside the creeper forest.," said the demon, "and so I shall give you a present."

Her eyes opened wide.

"What would you like to have?"

"Uh, I would, uh . . . ."

"Whatever you'd like, just ask."

"A necklace with a picture of Unnikrishnan in the locket," she shyly informed him.

This was a wish she'd held close to her heart for a long time. Many times she had told her mother and father about it, but to no avail. They would say: "You already have a diamond chain and a necklace, don't you? What do you need more jewelry for?"

One day when her father was in a good mood, he said, "I'll get you that necklace with the image of God inside. For your wedding . . . ."

"When would my wedding be?" she wondered. "My father insisted that I study at least until I got my B.A. Only after that would the question of marriage arise. How could I wait until then?"

The demon went inside. He returned with the necklace she requested. He placed it in the palm of her hand. It must weigh at least three pavans, she thought to herself.

She put the necklace around her neck. The demon helped her fasten the clasp.

And so it was that the most precious wish of her life had been fulfilled.

Exiting the forest of creeping vines, she ran home. She never got the seventh flower. Nevertheless, she was jubilant. Hadn't she seen a demon after all? Hadn't she been to his castle? Hadn't she received the necklace?

The locket that contained a picture of the resting Unnikrishnan hung on her chest on top of her red blouse. She kissed it.

"Where have you been, young lady? Tell me the truth." She was startled by her mother's voice.

"I just went to pick flowers. Remember?"

"Then where are the flowers?"

She had forgotten her flower basket in demon's castle.

"And what is this?"

Her mother's eyes fixed on her chest.

"Who gave you that? Tell the truth. I'll tear it to pieces."

"A demon."

Her mother stared at her.

"Really, Mother. A demon from the creeper forest gave it to me."

Her father came out from inside the house.

"Did you see this?" her mother turned to her father. "Seems a demon gave it to her."

"Who is this demon? What's his name?" asked her father. "Is it that moneybag's son from the big house? Is he your demon?"

Her head ached when she heard what her father said. She had heard the stories, too, about how the millionaire's son from the big house would buy girls jewelry.

"It's the truth, Dad, what I'm saying. He's a real demon, the king of the creeper forest . . . ."

She couldn't finish her sentence before she was felled by a slap.

Her father put her in her room and locked it from the outside. They didn't give her anything to eat or drink.

"Never until today has a girl from this family brought such shame on our name. I just want to . . . ."

On the other side of the locked door, she knew her father was enraged.

How many times did he slap her again and again? How many times did he lock her in her room? He starved her . . . .

No one believed that a demon, the king of the creeper forest, had given her the necklace.

Tears streamed down both of her cheeks. He slid off the necklace that clung to her white blouse with shining stars of golden silk. He put Unnikrishnan in his palm and touched him softly, saying:

"I believe you."

The Train That Had Wings

My wife is a beautiful woman with big hair, black eyes, and small breasts.

After our wedding, we spent a few days living it up in Madras before heading back to Delhi, where I work. We stayed on the third floor of a hotel on Wall Tax Road. Through the opened window, we could see the roof of the city—the roof forged of tile and concrete—slumping from the sky to the horizon. We slept the whole, hot day. Madras days are for sleep. And the nights are sleepless. The days in Madras are dark. And the sun shines at night. The dark, cold sun burns above the ocean at night. And the black sunlight rains over the city. The daytime sun sets and a hot, fiery shadow that yellows the eye, a flame-licked darkness spreads across the city.

We showered in the evening. She put on her Kanchipuram sari and drew thick tails next to her eyes. Finally, she donned a crown of jasmine flowers. She had become a *Tamil* girl!

"From now on, you are not allowed to speak Malayalam or English."

"Then what am I supposed to speak?"

"Chaste Tamil."

"Couldn't we just speak Celibate Malayalam or Immaculate English?"

We left the hotel and stepped out into the city.

We walked along Wall Tax Road.

We walked along Mount Road.

We walked along the endless Ponnamallee High Road.

We saw the Tamil girls with crowns of jasmine flowers. We saw the Anglo-Indian girls dressed in tiny frocks. The umbra of disease shone on their bastard faces. We saw the lepers, naked from head to toe, lying on the sidewalks, weeping. We saw the distorted faces of syphilitic beggars riddled with pustular sores. And we saw the living lumps of elephantiasis.

There are Tamil girls with jasmine flowers in their hair in Madras. There are no Tamil girls with jasmine flowers in their hair in Delhi.

There are lepers, naked from head to toe, in Madras.

There are people with syphilis and elephantiasis in Madras.

There are no people with elephantiasis in Delhi. There are people with syphilis.

The people with syphilis in Delhi do not lie around on the sidewalks; they do not lie down naked in the scorching sunlight; they do not beg. In Delhi, the people with syphilis wear three-piece suits, smoke pipes, drink imported liquor, and travel around in cars as big as cargo ships.

Madras is Delhi naked. Delhi is Madras in a three-piece suit.

We walked along the coast. Because it was Sunday, the city had poured itself onto the beach. The beach had become the city. From within the ocean, the watery waves crested and crashed. From the sands, from within the innumerable sands, the human waves crested and crashed. The scent of a thousand young girls filled the shoreline. The scent of a hundred thousand blooms of jasmine.

Madras is the city of jasmine.

As we walked through the human sea, it was as though I was not there. I began to question who I was. I was living a children's riddle, a Mother Goose tale. It seemed that humans did not exist or that the only thing existing was humans. She, too, must have been lost in a million thoughts, because she asked, "Do you know what I like to look at more than anything?"

"A Che Guevara film."

"No."

"The *Red Book*."

"Not that either."

"The setting sun."

"Uh-uh."

"The rising sun."

"No."

"Me."

"Uh-uh."

"Then what?"

"A crowd. A space packed with people as far as the eye can see."

Just people is not enough. They should have red flags in their hands and Maoist slogans on their lips.

"I like sprawled out crowds, too."

"Not as much as I do."

"More than you."

"No way. Not in a million years."

Then I remembered. In her room, on the floor, around the table, she had drawn sketches of crowds in all her books and notebooks. I guess what she said was true.

As she stood there watching the sea of people extending endlessly along Marina Beach, she said, "God, I feel crazy!"

As night encroached, the crowd began to melt away. The merchants, magicians, jugglers, and handbillers left the seaside. To the city, to the outskirts of the city, they returned. The lovers, male and female, returned. The fallen, crying beggars lying on the breast of the earth dozed off. My wife sadly sighed as the beach emptied. We walked dejectedly along the crowd-less seashore, thinking about the disassembled horde. The cavalry traveled along the beach hunting sleepers. Sleeping is not permitted on the beach. If it were, we would have slept there, too. Among the millions of footprints, breathing the footprints' odor, we would have gotten drunk and slept.

As we walked along the abandoned streets, I said, "I was dreaming about a crowd, too. But, there's one difference."

"What's that?"

She looked at my face.

"I saw red flags in their hands."

This is not my tragedy alone. This is the tragedy of our times.

It was one o'clock by the time we got back to our Wall Tax Road hotel. I opened the window and stood watching the sleeping city. If the world has any beauty at all, it could only be at night. In the daytime, the world shows its raw face. It casts off its clothes and exposes its naked body covered with festering ulcers. With a sinister grin, it parades before us. The world we see at night is a different one. In the bluish darkness, in the soft moonlight, the night envelopes us with its decorative stars, gentle breezes, and silence—this is the world I like.

"Me, too," she said. "Let's live like jackals. When we get to Delhi, let's sleep all day and live all night."

"How will I go to the office?"

"Why do you have to go there?"

How can we live without money?

"Even birds, animals, trees . . . "

" . . . don't go to the office." She finished my sentence.

A servant knocked on the door and entered. "Something to eat?"

We weren't very hungry. I had a tea. She ate some ice cream.

"I love to eat ice cream late at night."

After finishing our tea and ice cream, we lay down. I would not let her change out of her Kanchipuram sari or remove the flowers from her hair. This girl wrapped in the silk sari and wearing a crown of flowers is all mine! I couldn't believe it. I touched her beautiful neck, her conchlike ears and her eyelids trimmed with black ink. As I held her tightly in my thin arms, I whispered, "You're mine; mine alone."

～

We had to get up in the morning to see him. He was downstairs waiting for us. He wore a batting shirt and pajama bottoms. He had grown his hair into a jungle. A cigarette glowed in the lips.

I was very surprised when I saw him.

I hugged him and kissed his face.

"So, you're alive, eh?" his voice tripped out.

I had not run into him in six years. He had changed dramatically in that time. He used to be a thin, fair, and handsome man. Now he was fat. His eyes were red. His beauty was gone.

"Are you a hippie now, or what?"

"I'm still me. Only my body has changed."

"Aren't we just bodies?"

"You haven't lost your materialism yet, I see."

"Do you believe in God now?"

"Yeah, and God in me."

I took him to my room and introduced my wife to him.

"No defects, it seems," he said as he looked my wife up and down.

I introduced him to my wife, "This is an old friend of mine. He's the most daring Surrealist painter in India today."

She: "Not Dali?"

He: "No, not Dali, André Breton."

Me: "Are you Dada?"

From his colorful shirt he pulled out three fingers of pot, lit them up, and filled his pipe with the smoking leaves. Then he smoked away and told us his story.

◈

In the middle of college, he quit school and went off to see his country. Through the paddy fields of Andhra, across the wastelands of Maharashtra, through the thickets of Madhya Pradesh, through the deserts of Rajasthan, and among the sepulchers of Delhi and Agra—he wandered. He suffered the pains of starvation. He survived smallpox and yellow fever. He was ready to die. Finally, he was incarnated as a Surrealist painter in the artist's colony called *Cholamandalam,* in Madras. From Madras, he went to Europe. He debated Chagal and existentialism with the whores of Paris. He had sex with beautiful men.

His paintings can be seen in the world's best art galleries.

Yet, he was still starving.

"Have you got syphilis?" he asked.

"No, unfortunately."

"Then you're not a man."

"I've got a reproduction of Chagal's *Blue Violin*," she said.

"Do you like Surrealism?" he asked, "If so, I'll draw something for you."

"I don't want a Surrealist painting."

"Then what?"

"A painting of an ocean of people that never ends."

"What do you want in their hands? Mao's thoughts or Debray's revolution?"

A crowd without red flags just isn't complete.

He tapped out the ashes from his pipe. And putting it back in his pocket, he said, "Let's go to my mansion."

Without bathing, brushing our teeth, or drinking our morning tea, we went with him. I watched him with fascination. These fat, hairy legs of his had trudged across continents. Jumped over oceans. This long, stooped, fat body carries the scent of European prostitutes. These chapped lips bear the burn scars of marijuana and LSD. As I looked at him, I realized I was seeing the face of the times, the times in which we live.

Our taxi flew outside the city.

"What do you have to say about Europe?"

"Europe is just now beginning its existence. After the May Revolution in Paris, that is. Up to then, Europe was a fucking desert."

"Oh, you're exaggerating."

"No. Up to May 1968, Europe was a fucking desert. A desert populated by snobs, pseudointellectuals, and pseudowhores. Europe is a sham. Their existentialism is bullshit. No whitey has ever said anything that wasn't already said in the *Gita*."

"Europhobia," my wife diagnosed.

"It's better than Euromania, isn't it?" he retorted.

Our taxi stopped in front of his house. A golden-haired

young woman in a sari was standing there. He introduced us, "My woman. I married her when I was in Berlin. It was a love marriage."

Entering the house, he continued, "Even though I found her in Berlin, she's no Anglo-Saxon. She's a daughter of the Seine River."

The daughter of the Seine River and my wife introduced themselves.

I looked all around his house. I was struck dumb when I saw a train with wings flying through the air.

My wife said, "This isn't Surrealism. It's fantasy."

"Where do you draw the line?" the daughter of the Seine River joked.

"Which part of your wife's body do you like the most?" he asked.

"Her hair."

"Bullshit," he said as he spit on the floor and shot me a look of disgust.

"Which part do you like?"

Without pausing to think for even a moment, "Her tits."

The hot sun did not penetrate his house. It was cold and damp. His stuffed his pipe with weed. We passed it around, all smoking from the same pipe. The house filled with the stench and haze of pot. We didn't eat anything. We lay on the floor, in the thin darkness, in the smoke. Stroking my wife's hair, he said, "You were right. She's got great hair . . . "

"Not just her hair. I also like her hands."

Now embracing my wife, he said, "Your wife is a flower."

"Where's the Nihilist, the Surrealist in you?"

"I've never denied beauty."

As evening approached, we started to get hungry. I woke up the daughter of the Seine River who was sleeping in my arms. The four of us went outside. We looked at the world. The blue sky was bluer. The beautiful jasmine was more beautiful. The humid air was wetter.

Together we sat around the table and ate. We went to the

beach. We wandered through each and every street. We slept in the same room together. The Seine River flowed through my arms. He interrupted his sleep at night to paint my wife's por-trait . . .

We spent hours and hours tripping on pot . . .

On the fifth day, my wife and I said goodbye.

The Surrealist painters wandering around Delhi are waiting for us. The wandering, hash-eating hippies who fill up Delhi are waiting for us. The Delhi filled with sepulchers awaits.

Let us go then.

Tonsured Life

It was a busy day of work at the office.

I removed my coat and hung it on the hanger. I rolled up my shirt sleeves above my elbows, took out a pen, and started to work. Of course then the phone rang. It was the girl from reception.

"Someone is here to see you."

"Who is it, dear?" I asked.

"A healthy, well-to-do man. Maybe forty or so."

"Didn't you ask his name?"

"Let me ask, dear."

He listened to her put the phone down. Not a second later, she inquired, "What is your name?"

"Lakshman-lal Pyari-lal Pandit-ji."

She laughed amid the phones ringing around her.

Who is this Lakshman-lal Pyari-lal Pandit-ji? I turned my chair around and thought for a moment. I had never met a person like this before. I don't have any experience with such people. Should I see him or not? I asked myself. I couldn't make up my mind, so I called down to the receptionist girl and asked:

"Do I want to see Lakshman-lal Pyari-lal Pandit-ji?"

"Yes, you do," she said.

Since she thought I should see him, I figured I would. I mean I had slept with her the night before, right? The fragrance of shampoo in her hair still lingered in the seat of my intellect.

I put my jacket back on. Combed my hair. Straightened my tie. Lit my pipe, took a big puff, and went to reception. In the red cushion of a cane chair in the reception area sat Pandit-ji reading the *Bhagavad-Gita*. When I saw that he was reading the *Bhagavad-Gita*, I continued to be totally confused.

"My name is . . . "

I introduced myself. Lakshman-lal Pyari-lal Pandit-ji raised his head from his book and looked me over. His eyes had a uniqueness about them. For some reason, I just couldn't face those eyes. My head lowered.

Closing his *Gita*, Pandit-ji stood up. It was then that I realized how unusually tall he was.

"Come—" he said.

"To where?"

Pandit-ji's expression suddenly changed. His eyes turned fierce.

"Didn't I tell you to come—"

He walked outside. For a moment I stood there stunned. After drawing on my pipe, I followed him without taking the pipe from my mouth. I didn't fear him—or anyone. Let me see what Pandit-ji's up to.

Trailing Pandit-ji, I exited the office.

In front of the office waited two chenda drummers, a barber, and an ass, not to mention a few other people. It was as though they were all waiting for me.

Next to the chenda drummers were their massive drums.

The ass was wizened and feeble.

Pandit-ji waved over the barber. The barber approached us.

"Sit down over there—" Pandit-ji ordered.

I had never heard such a voice before. Lost in the depth of that voice, I had sat down without knowing it.

"Don't move," Pandit-ji warned.

What happened after that, I am not exactly sure. I lost consciousness. I was in a kind of hypnotic trance. My brain was no longer my brain. My eyes were no longer my eyes. The blood in my veins flowed outside of me. Flowing through another's veins, my body was released from my body.

I was lost to myself, and I passed from myself to the outside.

The pipe I was smoking fell from my mouth.

The barber tiptoed in front of me. He removed his weapons from a leather bag. A long, sharp blade with a piercingly bright edge, soap, a towel. And he had readied a little water in his aluminum bowl.

"Move over and sit here," demanded the barber.

I moved over. I was unable at that moment to refuse even his commands. Am I not better than a barber?

The barber grabbed my head and squeezed it between his palms. My head that yesterday rested on the breast of my young receptionist, my head that had tramped through so many young women, had crafted so many paintings, had toiled over so many poems . . .

My head that rested crooked and squished in my mother's womb . . .

My head that must tomorrow pop and crackle in the fire of Delhi's electric crematorium . . .

My head, my everything . . .

My head that in lives to come must ornament the serpents, bear the beasts, and sustain the worms . . .

Part of the snakes, part of the beasts, part of the birds, my head that must bear witness for my future lives . . .

On that head the barber sprinkled water from his aluminum bowl. And on that head moved the barber's razor-sharp blade . . .

The hair that I nurtured with shampoo and Silvikrin, that I guarded like gold, my hair . . .

Pandit-ji stood with his hands clasped behind his back, watching the barber perform the tonsure.

The barber's blade journeyed repeatedly along my head. I felt the razor-sharp blade move across my naked skull. There must have been nicks here and there, even though I didn't feel any pain.

The barber's blade moved not along my skull but along my heart. What he twisted and tore was not my hair. It was my soul.

That knife traveled over my bones; over the marrow and the fat; over my nerves . . .

What the barber tonsured was my life. From here on mine is a shorn life. A hairless, naked, scar-filled life.

When the barber finished his task, Pandit-ji ordered:

"Get up."

I obeyed. My legs trembled as I stood. Beads of sweat dripped down my head and neck. Beads of blood. Blood, not sweat, flowed through my hair follicles.

The barber rubbed his blade clean and put it in his leather pouch. He emptied the aluminum bowl and packed it, too.

Pandit-ji scoured me all over with his stare. Then he made some gesture with his eyes.

A kid wearing dirty, foul-smelling pants moved next to the ass. Guiding the ass, he stopped in front of me. The ass looked at me with suffering eyes.

Weren't those my eyes?

Wasn't I that ass?

"Get on," decreed Pandit-ji.

I looked back and forth from the ass to Pandit-ji. How does one climb on the back of an ass? I didn't know. I knew how to drive a scooter. But until now, I'd never mounted an ass or a horse.

"Didn't I tell you to get on—"

Fire shot from Pandit-ji's eyes.

I moved near the ass, threw my arms around it, and somehow managed to climb onto its back. Hunched over, I squeezed its neck tightly in order to not fall off.

What would happen if I did fall?

I have fallen: into the pit of hell. I am in a roaring fire. I am in gurgitating ghee. I am in the middle of entwined serpents, dancing and writhing and spewing their venom.

From here on, there was no refuge for me; as I boiled in the fire, I became the fire. As I softened in the ghee, I became the ghee. As I bore the snake bite, I became the venom.

Nothing will be nothing.

When I sat down on the back of the ass, Pandit-ji stared

straight at the chenda drummers. They strapped their chendas, and perumbara drums to their necks. They took their drumsticks in hand.

The beats on the skin of the chenda rang out.

"Walk—" Pandit-ji said to everyone.

He walked in front. Behind the chenda drummers, and behind them me, sitting on the back of an ass. Behind me, blowing whistles, some beggars sang dirty songs.

And so from the front of my office, the festival procession chugged forward.

It was midday. Tons of people were on the street. People crowded all the cars and the buses. Wouldn't someone I know be in the crowd? Surely so.

My friends.

The fans who read my poems.

The art lovers who paid top price for my paintings.

All the young women I've slept with . . . they would all see my tonsured head. They would see me traveling on the back of an ass. They would see the chenda drummers serving as my bodyguards. They would see the beggars anointing me with their parodies . . . .

Between the renovated shops that lined the main street, amidst the men and women, the mothers and daughters, through the children, the festival procession pushed forward.

An old man dressed in a white dhoti hurled an insult my way between the crunches and chaws of his paan: "Motherfucker."

Another man peeled his sandal off his foot and threw it at my head. And that sandal with a broken strap, smeared with shit, did indeed land on my head . . . .

About an hour passed, the ass panted as it walked, the chenda drummers bathed in sweat.

As we came to a tea stall, Pandit-ji turned and said:
"Stop!"

The drummers stopped beating the chendas. The whistle blowers and insult hurlers became silent.

"Bring us some tea, friend," Pandit-ji said to the shopkeeper. Pandit-ji, the barber, and the others all sat in the chairs out-side the stall. I thought he would tell me to sit, too. But it didn't happen. Without saying a word, Pandit-ji sat with his legs crossed in his chair. He opened up a book and started to read.

I noticed that it was the *Bible*.

The shopkeeper brought the tea in glasses. He distributed to each his own. I longed for him to give me a glass as well. My throat was parched with thirst.

But, as the shopkeeper extended a glass to me, Pandit-ji pre-vented him:

"Don't give him anything."

A young boy wearing soiled pants brought some water in a bucket and gave it to the ass. If I could just get a little of that water . . . .My throat filled with flame. If I could only get a sin-gle drop of water to douse that flame . . . .

"Water—" I cried from the ass's back. The shopkeeper looked back and forth from Pandit-ji to me. Pandit-ji shook his head to indicate no.

After finishing their tea, they sat for a time and rested. Pandit-ji opened another book and started reading. This time it was the *Koran*.

He carried several books with him. Books on religion, phi-losophy, law . . . .

The tea and the rest break complete, Pandit-ji stood up.

"Let's move!" he commanded. The drummers got up, took their chendas, and draped them over their necks. The beggars put out their cigarettes and began to blow their whistles and shout their profanities.

The festival procession pushed forward again.

From one street to another, from one subdivision to anoth-er, the parade continued. Pandit-ji and the drummers ate some dinner, and several times they had tea and cold drinks.

They gave me no dinner, no tea, no cold drink.

Not even a little drinking water.

What good was food to me now? What good was tea? What good a cold drink?

What use was water?

As the early evening approached, the festival procession reached the old city. At the same moment, my shaven head beamed out in the light of dusk. My whole body, my rotten egg, my putrid skin itched and burned.

As dusk fell, our festival parade came to an end. The chendas became silent, the drummers, the barber, and the others went their separate ways.

Even the ass went away.

When it was all over, when everyone had gone, it was just me and Lakshman-lal Pyari-lal Pandit-ji. We were near the Red Fort. In the distance you could see the lights of Chandni Chowk. Dim stars above the Red Fort.

I was a total wreck, spent by all the abuse, the hunger, and the thirst. You could say that I was unconscious. I could barely move my tongue. But, wetting my lips, I struggled to ask Pandit-ji what I had wanted to ask all along:

"Why this punishment, Pandit-ji?"

Pandit-ji mumbled on hearing my question, as though I had no right to be asking questions. As though I had no right to speak at all.

"Tell me, Pandit-ji," I repeated, mustering up all my strength as I teetered between consciousness and unconsciousness.

"You want to know? Then listen well."

Pandit-ji turned and faced me straight on. I was lying face down on the ground.

"One day an old man was thirsty. He came to your house and said, 'I need some water, please.' Do you remember, you dirty bastard?"

"Yes, I remember it clearly."

It was a Sunday. The hottest part of the day. I was sitting in the chair on my balcony reading the poems of Otto Castillo. The old man approached. He must have been seventy or eighty years old, a beggar with withered, bony arms. His face was blistered by the sun and sweat dripped down his neck.

"Water! . . . . . . " pleaded the run-down old man, holding on to the gate, "A little water! . . . . "

The old man's voice was pitiful like any cry of distress. This I could tell right away. I took the tall glass that I usually drink beer from and filled it to the top with cold water from the fridge.

I helped the old man onto the verandah and gave him a seat. He didn't have the strength in his arms to hold the glass, so I helped him put the glass to his mouth. Painfully he drank down the water, three or four glassfuls . . . .

After resting a while he thanked me with his two hands and left.

"Why did you give this man water? Who are you to give water to the thirsty?"

Pandit-ji's eyes glowed with rage. He hawked his phlegm and spit in my face. He lifted his hand as if to strike me. Then he turned and walked off toward the lights of Chandni Chowk.

I remained there, lying in the dark.

Delhi 1981

Rajinder Pande opened the window and looked outside. Row after row of shops lined the sides of the street. Behind the shops, he could see a large field. From the street, you couldn't see the field, but his room was located on the second floor facing the street. And so, standing near the window, he could clearly see the street and row of shops below and field just beyond.

A footpath cut through the middle of the field that could easily be used to reach the main road leading to Chirag Delhi. The field was usually deserted. Only rarely would it happen that someone would actually come or go using the footpath. Sometimes during the day, pigs would walk through there grazing. On the western side there was a dilapidated old tomb from the time of the Mughals. The graveyard was thick with pigeons. The sound of the pigeons' cooing and flapping their wings was always audible.

Pande stood there just staring outside as he held the sides of the window frame. Along with him, Kishore Lal, who lived there in the same room, was listening to a song on the radio. Pande, who never liked film songs, got bored and without realizing it ended up in front of the window.

He saw Raghuvir and Nanak Chand walking along the street below. They were the big local thugs. Both were young.

Raghuvir had spent two days in jail for harassing some girls from I. P. College at their bus stop. Nanak Chand had been to jail a total of five times. The last time was for swiping some jewelry from a woman's neck.

Pande watched as Raghuvir and Nanak Chand went down behind Amir Singh's dry cleaning store toward the field. The two sat down on a cut rock as they smoked.

At a distance on the other side of the field, Pande noticed a yellowish shadow appearing. And with it a long shadow. A few seconds later he realized that it was a woman in a yellow sari and a man. And just then he also saw a baby in the man's arms.

From the rock where they sat, Raghuvir turned his head to look at the woman and man. Then he said something to Nanak Chand. He, too, turned to look at the couple. Again they said something to each other. They got up and began to walk through the field.

"Hey, Kishore, you wanna see something funny? Come here."

Rajinder Pande called Kishore Lal to the window. Kishore Lal put his finger to his lips, telling Pande to be quiet. On the radio, Amitabh Bacchan was singing something from *Lovers*.

Arms on each other's shoulders, they were casually walking through the middle of the field—Nanak Chand and Raghuvir, passing a single cigarette back and forth. The yellowish shadow became clearer now. The woman and man had almost reached the center of the field. Pande couldn't see her face clearly from where he stood at the window. Still he surmised that she was attractive. The man who walked with her was tall and thin. Mother, Father, and Baby—they were a complete, perfect family.

It must have been because the sun was so strong that the woman covered her head with the end of her sari. They had come to the middle of the field.

Nanak Chand and Raghuvir's pace slowed. As far as the eye could stretch, no one else could be seen anywhere near the field. Even the pigeons in the run-down tomb were silent.

"Hey, Kishore. Turn the radio off and come over here, man." Pande once again called Kishore Lal over to the window.

Nanak Chand and Raghuvir drew near the little family.

"Dude, get your ass up and get over here."

Pande stared out at the center of the field. Kishore Lal stood up and came to the window without turning the radio off.

Raghuvir and Nanak Chand blocked the path. Nanak Chand put both of his hands in his back pockets. He stared and laughed at the young woman without taking the cigarette from his mouth. The young man's face reddened.

"Please step aside, you thugs," he said, "Jerks—"

Nanak Chand and Raghuvir didn't react at all to what he said. The young woman pulled her yellow sari across her face and stood there cringing. Both her cheeks became red with unease.

"Man, what do you think Nanak Chand and Raghuvir are gonna do?" Kishore Lal asked Pande.

"Let's wait and see. Give me a cigarette, yaar."

Kishore Lal pulled a packet of Red & Whites from his pocket and held one out for Pande. Each of them lit up a cigarette and watched the field with increasing interest. The sunlight was boiling hot there.

"They're gonna have to move them somewhere, man." Pande declared. But where could they go at this time of day, in this heat?

"Hey, yellow bird, let us see your pretty face."

Nanak Chand pulled the young woman's sari from her face. Full, fleshy cheeks, blooming eyes, an astonishingly beautiful face. Kumkum powder graced the part in the middle of her hair. A bindi on her forehead.

Nanak Chand turned straight to the young man with a baby in his arms and said, "Hey brother, you're a lucky guy. Got yourself a wife just like Hemamalini."

The young man's patience was dwindling. He was burning up inside. His baby in his arms. His wife with him. Otherwise. . . .

He suppressed his rage and said softly, "Friends, what do you want? It's not right to behave so indecently. You're educated young men, aren't you? Please . . . let us by."

Pressing the baby close to his chest, he grabbed his wife's hand and tried to go around them.

"Hey, don't be in such a rush."

Raghuvir put his hand on the young man's shoulder.

"Without our permission you don't move from this spot, got it?"

The young man quickly braced his hand, speared a glance at Raghuvir, and gave him a slap. The baby cradled in his arms began to cry.

"You fuckin' bastard. You think you're all that, huh?"

Nanak Chand pulled a knife from inside his pants and flashed it. The young woman's heart beat like a bird's. With her eyes she pleaded with her husband not to do anything that might make things worse.

The young man put his child in his wife's arms and stood ready for anything.

"Fuckin' bastard—"

Raghuvir rubbed the sting from his slapped face, turned and grabbed the young man by his shirt. Cradling the crying baby in her arms, the young woman desperately looked around for help. She shook with fear from head to toe.

"One more cigarette, yaar."

Pande extended his hand to Kishore without taking eyes off the field. He lit another cigarette and took a puff. Through the smoke, he said:

"Yaar . . . very interesting."

As the young man and Nanak Chand brawled with kicks and punches, Raghuvir walked away a short distance and returned with a big rock in his hands. He stood there hands over head holding the big rock over the young man's skull. On seeing that, the yellow bird fainted in a slump.

From the other side of the field appeared a white shadow. A middle-aged gentleman covered with bulbous tumors. He was carrying a briefcase. Staring at the middle of the field, he paused confusedly for a moment. Then, briefcase in full swing, he continued walking toward them.

"Who the hell is that guy?" Pande said. The newcomer would be a total buzzkill. He'll wreck everything, Pande thought.

The young man and Nanak Chand continued to argue, pushing and shoving each other. Raghuvir still held the rock in his hand. He kept holding it over the young man's head, torturing the paralyzed young woman.

When she saw the gentleman walking through the field, she sucked in a quick breath.

"Help us! Please come quickly . . . They're going to kill my baby's father . . . ." she screamed at the top of her lungs.

The gentleman started to run over. His burdened body shook as he rushed toward the young woman. When the gentleman was about a hundred yards away, Raghuvir turned toward him:

"Get the fuck out of here, asshole."

Raghuvir aimed the rock in his hand directly at him. The gentleman's legs suddenly couldn't move. He noticed the knife with the long blade in Nanak Chand's hand.

"Get outta here . . . fuck off."

Pausing for a moment, the gentleman then turned away, ignoring the young's woman's pleas for help.

"Get the fuck out!"

The gentleman geared up his fat frame and ran off, briefcase in hand.

"Bravo!" laughed Pande and Kishore as they stood at the window.

At that moment, Raghuvir lifted the rock high and slammed it down on the young man's head. His legs started to buckle beneath him. Nanak Chand lifted his leg and kicked him in the gut. With that, he collapsed forward like a bending bow and fell down face first.

"I can't get enough of this Nanak Chand and Raghuvir.

Really great, okay, yaar?" Kishore Lal said that last part in English.

Pande replied, "Very, very great, okay, yaar."

Both of their eager eyes on the center of the field.

"Get up, sister." Nanak Chand grabbed the arm of the young woman as she wept near her husband.

"We've got a little surprise for you in that tomb over there . . . "

He pointed a finger toward the decaying tomb nearby.

"Please don't hurt me."

Her eyes filled with tears, her hands folded in supplication.

Nanak Chand yanked her up hard and pushed her forward. The tiny baby lay on the ground crying out. Raghuvir quickly took out a handkerchief from his pocket and shoved it in the baby's mouth. The baby's eyes bulged out. Its crying ceased.

The young woman wrested herself free and started to run through the field.

"Grab her, you stupid fuck!"

Nanak Chand fumed. Raghuvir raced after her and caught her. Together the two of them dragged her toward the tomb. From the top of the crumbling walls of the tomb watched a group of agitated pigeons.

"It's all right, dude, they're taking her off to rape her," Kishore Lal said. They watched the field as though they were watching a film in Eastman cinemascope.

Both Raghuvir and Nanak Chand forced her inside the tomb. They ripped off the yellow bird's sweat-soaked yellow blouse. They threw her up against the crumbling stone wall. At this point, she had no strength left to fight back. Her head simply slumped to one side.

"Who's gonna be first, you think?" asked Kishore Lal.

"Nanak Chand, of course," said Pande.

Raghuvir held her up against the wall. Nanak Chand undid the buttons on his pants . . . .

At that moment, Rajinder Pande's room takes the form of a large city. Buildings that touch the sky rise up. Rajinder Pande and Kishore Lal become a population of five and a half million people. Standing on raised platforms, amidst the booming cheers, dressed in white homespun and Gandhi caps, the leaders deliver Hindi harangues without breaths or breaks. Sitting around tables in coffeehouses laden with cigarette smoke, carrying their shoulder bags, the long-haired, long-bearded literati debate . . .

At that moment, a young pigeon flies up from the darkness of the tomb and begins to peck and poke with its tender beak at the head of Nanak Chand . . . .

O Prostitutes, A Temple for You

He made sure to take a prostitute with him whenever he went to Haridwar.

Every day prostitutes would come by his house. At the office, meanwhile, call girls usually answered the phones. In restaurants, it was with hookers that he usually drank his coffee. Whenever he went to a gallery to see an exhibition, whores would accompany him. Going to worship at the Hanuman temple he was always in the company of prostitutes.

There would probably be prostitutes with him on his trip to the funeral pyre.

His life was a roadside temple for whores.

The greatest tragedy of his life was the fact that he hadn't been born in the belly of a prostitute; instead he had to pop out of the womb of a mother of impeccable character and reputable family. Except for his father, not a single other man's seed had entered this womb—and in this womb he had taken shape in blood, in bone, and in flesh; that itself was a tragedy.

Napoleon, Che Guevara, and Bob Dylan all suffered the same tragedy. Erwin Strittmatter and Witold Gombrowicz hung from the crosses of the same tragedy. The tragedy of Buddha and of Jesus was indeed his tragedy.

Why weren't Napoleon, Che Guevara, and Bob Dylan born in the womb of a prostitute?

Why weren't Strittmatter and Gombrowicz children of whores?

Why didn't Lord Buddha and Lord Jesus assume their existence in the belly of a harlot?

He was not born in the womb of a prostitute. It was true. But he did live with prostitutes. And he would probably croak while cuddling them in his arms. Yes, he would only die in the company of a whore.

It was certain that a prostitute would accompany him to Haridwar.

Shanta the Harlot of Karol Bagh said:

"I too am coming to Haridwar."

Shanta was from Trishnapalli. She was dark and thin. She was also a cripple.

Kanta the Whore of Darya Ganj asked:

"Can I come too?"

Kanta was not from Trishnapalli. She was not dark and thin. She was not a cripple.

Kanta was not Shanta.

Kanta was Panjabi. She was the color of wheat. She always rubbed mustard oil in her hair before she brushed it.

Kanta was Kanta.

Shanta was Shanta.

Kanta was Kanta and Shanta was Shanta.

Lata from Defense Colony was eighteen. She spoke English like a Yankee. She was a Beatles fan, she wore bell-bottoms and a go-go shirt; she had a nose ring.

Lata the Prostitute said:

"I too shall come."

She wouldn't come for no reason. You had to pay her. She got paid by the minute. Her price for an hour was seventy-five rupees. They had made plans to spend three days in Haridwar.

"How much do you want?"

"How about five hundred?"

"Okay."

Lata was enough. Her nose ring was enough. Her blossoming buttocks were enough. Five hundred rupees was like fodder. Ten days wages. Not just ten days wages, he would give her a month's wages. He would give her a year's wages. He would give her a salary for her whole lifetime.

You are enough. Your nose ring is enough.

"Is five hundred too much?"

"No, too little."

"How about a thousand then?"

"I'd give you ten thousand."

Ten thousand was an elephant's price. Whores don't command an elephant's price!

"If you have it, I know you'll give it."

She laughed like the ring of a telephone. She loved him. His powerful arms and legs, his long neck, his broad chest, his lips stained with pipe smoke—she loved it all.

She was not the only one who loved him.

Shanta of Karol Bagh loved him, too.

But Shanta was not the only one who loved him.

Kanta of Darya Ganj loved him, too.

But Lata, Shanta, and Kanta were not the only ones who loved him. All the prostitutes in the city loved him.

He was a temple for prostitutes.

Man has built temples for the demon king Ravanan. He has built temples throughout the land to the monkey Hanuman. He has installed and worshiped the piss pipe of Shiva.

No one has built a temple for the prostitutes.

He will build one. He has built temples for them throughout his life in every quarter.

O Eunuchs from the Triveni Ghats, sing your Gayatri mantras for the prostitutes.

O Temple Priests, make your holy offerings for the prostitutes.

O Temple Bells, ring for the prostitutes.

O Sacred Lamps, burn for the prostitutes.

O World, shed your tears for the prostitutes who bestow happiness on mankind again and again even as they meet their venereal-diseased death in the putrid sewers of society. Prostitutes are angels. Suffering ascetics. Goddesses. O prostitutes, I cry out for you.

"Where shall I meet you?"

He heard Lata's voice again on the phone.

"Get everything ready and wait at the house. Six o'clock in the morning."

He packed up his shirt and pants in a suitcase. All the necessary knicks and knacks including some after shave and eau de cologne. A large can of tobacco and three pipes.

He locked the suitcase and called a taxi. The taxi said:

"Two minutes, sir."

When he locked his room and came outside, the taxi was already there.

"Where to?" the taxi asked.

"Defense Colony."

"Which block?" the taxi queried as it ran.

"The block where Lata the Whore lives."

The taxi then flew to Defense Colony with contempt on its lips stained red from the pan it chewed. He knew Lata's house. And not just he, all the taxis knew it. And not just the taxis, the Cadillacs and the Chevrolets also knew her house. Her house was a pilgrimage shrine.

O Pilgrims, why do you go to Rishikesh? Dear Pilgrims, why do you descend in droves on Allahabad? O Pilgrims, why do you climb the hills at Amarnath and Badrinath?

Karol Bagh where Shanta lives is Rishikesh. Darya Ganj where Kanta lives is Badrinath. Defense Colony where Lata lives is Amarnath.

Lata was waiting on the verandah. The gaunt of little sleep was in her eyes. She was wrapped in a green sari. Teeth-marks reddened her cheeks.

"You know, just seeing you, I would never guess you were a prostitute."

"Then what would you think."

"That you're a goddess."

"I am a prostitute. My body reeks of sin."

"Your body has the aroma of immortal nectar."

She joined him on the seat.

"Did you sleep last night? How many customers did you have?"

"Two."

She described who they were. One was the deputy secretary from some embassy. He had whiskers the color of gold. The other was a well-known painter in the city. He had long hair.

"From someone's teeth?"

"The painter's."

Was the painter drawing pictures on her cheeks with his teeth?

The taxi drove to the New Delhi train office.

"Do you know why you're coming with me?"

"To satisfy your lust."

"No, to cleanse my sins."

⁓

Grasping Shanta's blackened and crippled leg, he sobbed:

"Please rescue me from my sins."

She cried.

"You are a goddess."

The goddess's eyes, riddled with venereal disease, burst into tears.

⁓

In their first-class compartment on the Mussoorie Express, he slept with his head resting on a prostitute's shoulder.

Holding a prostitute's hand, he got down in Haridwar.

"Do you have V.D.?"

"No, but soon enough."

She laughed.

O Holy Temples of Khajuraho, shackle me to your walls.

O Temple Dancers, rise up from your funeral pyres. Come and rewrite the destiny of your forehead in this Kali era. Come . . .

I am waiting.

Rise up from the exhaustion of your first lovemaking. He said:

"Let's go see Manasa Devi."

They changed their clothes and exited the terminal building. They walked along Upper Road. One has to climb a steep hill in order to reach Manasa Devi's presence. They climbed to the top in the tracks of innumerable others. Finally, the tracks stopped.

They went before Manasa Devi and worshiped her.

Great Goddess, I have not brought flowers for you. Neither have I any sweet-smelling offerings. Instead of flowers and sweet aromas, I have brought prostitutes more immaculate than any flower or incense. Please do me the honor of accepting them . . .

He walked along the crowded edge of the ghats holding the prostitute's hand.

She said:

"I would like to bathe."

Countless pilgrims were plunging themselves clean in the ghats. The river had become clouded with their sins. Fish fattened on the iniquity strutted and played in the water.

"Let me cleanse my sins here," she said again.

Why was she bathing in the Ganges? Was not she Ganga Devi herself?

Yes, please bathe. Let the Ganges receive liberation from sin by your touch. Let the Ganges be purified.

Beyond the Saptadharas, the river coursed with terrible roars and bellows.

"Let us bathe nude."

"What if someone sees?"

"Is there anyone who hasn't already seen you naked?"

O Seven Sages, by the footstep of Lata the Harlot the seven continents have been made pure.

O Sages, meditate on Lata.
O Brahmakunda, light your camphor flames for Lata.
"Come."
The river called.

Holding the hands of a prostitute, he entered the water. They traveled through the river. They passed the Saptadharas, passed Brahmakunda, through the legs of bridge after bridge, heading for the Bengal sea, they flowed.

Suggestions for Further Reading

Two of Mukundan's best novels have recently been translated into English (and one into French). Both depict life in Mukundan's native Mahe, a tiny former French colony in the present state of Kerala, and present an understanding of the colonial experience in India and the transition to independence not found elsewhere. These two novels established Mukundan as one of Malayalam literature's luminaries and are much loved by scholars and general readers alike.

Mukundan, M. *On the Banks of the Mayyazhi*. Trans. Gita Krishnankutty. Chennai: Manas, 1999.

———. *God's Mischief*. Trans. Prema Jayakumar. Delhi: Penguin, 2002.

———. *Sur les rives du fleuve Mahé*. Trans. Sophie Bastide-Foltz. Actes Sud, 2002.

Mukundan's work is, of course, best understood as part of the broader milieu of his generation of writers and as a response to the work of the preceding generations. Though many excellent works are not available in English, examples of nationalist and social realist works in English translation include the following.

Anterjanam, Laithambika. *Cast Me Out If You Will: Stories and Memoir.* Trans. Gita Krishnankutty. New York: The Feminist Press at CUNY, 1998.

Basheer, Vaikom Muhammad. *"Me grandad 'ad an elephant": Three Stories of Muslim Life in South India.* Trans. R. E. Asher. Edinburgh: Edinburgh University Press, 1980.

—————. *Poovan Banana and Other Stories.* Trans. V. Abdulla. New Delhi: Orient Longman, 1994.

Dev, P. Kesava. *Neighbours.* Trans. P. K. Ravindranath. New Delhi: Sahitya Akademi, 1979.

Kuttikrishnan, P. C. (Uroob). *Beloved.* Trans. Raghava R. Menon. Delhi: Hind Pocket Books, 1974.

—————. *The Beautiful and the Handsome.* Trans. Susheela Misra. Trichur: Kerala Sahitya Akademi, 1982.

Pillai, Thakazhi Sivasankara. *Chemmeen: A Novel.* Trans. Narayana Menon. New York: Harper. Reprint. 1979. Westport, CT: Greenwood Press, 1962.

—————. *Scavenger's Son.* Trans. R. E. Asher. London: Heinemann Educational, 1993.

Among the best translations of works by Mukundan's contemporaries are the following books.

Das, Kamala, *The Sandal Trees and Other Stories.* Trans. V. C. Harris and C. K. Mohammed Ummer. Bombay: Orient Longman, 1995.

Nair, M. T. Vasudevan. *The Demon Seed and Other Writings.* Trans. V. Abdulla and Gita Krishnankutty. New Delhi: Penguin, 1998.

—————. *Catching an Elephant and Other Stories.* Trans. V. Abdulla. Calcutta: Rupa & Co., 1991.

Sachidanandan, P. (Anand). *The Death Certificate: A Novel.* Trans. Gita Krishnankutty. Bombay: Sangam Books, 1983.

Sethu. *Pandavapuram.* Trans. Prema Jayakumar. New Delhi: Macmillan India, 1995.

Vijayan, O. V. *The Legends of Khasak.* trans. by the author. New Delhi: Penguin India, 1994.

—————. *After the Hanging and Other Stories*. trans. by the author. New Delhi: Penguin Books India, 1989.

Zacharia, Paul. *Bhaskara Pattelar and Other Stories*. trans. by the author. New Delhi: Manas, 1994.

An online bibliography of Malayalam literature in translation, including novels, short stories, poetry, anthologies, and secondary works through 1998 was created by Irene Joshi at the University of Washington:

http://www.lib.washington.edu/Southasia/guides/malayalam.html

No adequate survey of modern Malayalam literature exists in English. Otherwise useful surveys are not up to date and generally do not cover works after the early 1970s. The following secondary works are recommended with this caveat in mind.

Ayyappapaniker, K. P. *A Short History of Malayalam Literature*. 3rd rev. and enl. ed. Trivandrum: Dept. of Public Relations, 1982.

George, Karimpumannil Mathai. *A Survey of Malayalam Literature*. Bombay: Asia Publishing House, 1968.

Tharakan, K. M. *A Brief Survey of Malayalam Literature: History of Literature*. Kottayam: National Book Stall, 1990.

Though literary genres and practices changed dramatically in Kerala (and in India generally) during the British colonial period, some readers may be interested in the literary culture of early Kerala. The following recent work is highly recommended on this subject:

Rich Freeman. "Genre and Society: The Literary Culture of Premodern Kerala," in *Literary Cultures in History: Reconstructions from South Asia*. Ed. Sheldon Pollock. Berkeley: Univ. California Press, 2003.

www.ingramcontent.com/pod-product-compliance
Lightning Source LLC
Chambersburg PA
CBHW031206260626
47169CB00004B/1269